8/2019

(

ONLY THE
STUBBORN SURVIVE

Center Point
Large Print

Also by R. W. Stone and available from
Center Point Large Print:

Badman's Pass
Across the Rio Bravo
Canadian Red
Back with a Vengeance

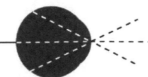

ONLY THE STUBBORN SURVIVE

R. W. Stone

CENTER POINT LARGE PRINT
THORNDIKE, MAINE

This Circle Ⓥ Western is published by
Center Point Large Print in the year 2019 in
co-operation with Golden West Literary Agency.

First Edition
July, 2019

Printed in the United States of America
on permanent paper.
Set in 16-point Times New Roman type.

ISBN: 978-1-64358-269-6

Library of Congress Cataloging-in-Publication Data

Names: Stone, R. W., author.
Title: Only the stubborn survive : a Circle V Western / R.W. Stone.
Description: Large Print edition. | First Edition. | Thorndike, Maine :
    Center Point Large Print, 2019. | Series: A Circle V Western
Identifiers: LCCN 2019016401 | ISBN 9781643582696 (hardcover :
    alk. paper)
Subjects: LCSH: Large type books. | GSAFD: Western stories.
Classification: LCC PS3619.T67 O55 2019 | DDC 813/.6—dc23
LC record available at https://lccn.loc.gov/2019016401

"Wars may be fought with weapons, but they are won by men. It is the spirit of the men who follow and of the man who leads that gains the victory."

General Patton
Cavalry Journal (9/33)

This book is dedicated to those who serve.
Like the Spartans at Thermopylae,
heroes stand their ground so that others may
continue to live in freedom.

PROLOGUE

A pair of horsemen rode silently across the barren landscape toward a far destination. Even though the prairie that surrounded them stretched out like a vast untamed ocean, these men did not veer from their course. Both of the riders were experienced and trail-wise. They knew all too well that while such terrain might appear flat and empty, it was merely an illusion.

Believing that in a great expanse of country such as this there would be ample time to spot any unexpected danger was tenderfoot thinking. Both of these two horsemen knew fully well there were hundreds of small arroyos, gullies, buffalo wallows, and plant-filled overgrowths that could easily hide an enemy. One who might be waiting to rob or, worse yet, kill and take one's scalp.

Perhaps to the inexperienced this pair might have appeared relaxed and unaware as they rode along, but nothing could have been further from the truth. Their slouched bodies were merely a Westerner's way of riding great distances on horseback without strain, and a closer look would have revealed that neither of the two men's eyes ever stopped moving. Both scanned the horizon, the ground in front of them, and their back trail, for not to do so out here often meant certain death.

One of the two riders was young and tall. His name was Red Smith. He was thin and clean shaven, with a head of red hair. He wore a smooth brown leather vest, a pinched-crown Stetson, and on his waist was a wide cartridge belt and tooled holster combination known by some as a buscadero rig. He was mounted on a chocolate roan, a term often used to describe this horse's unique coloration. His cayuse had a solid rusty brown mane and tail, but the rest of the animal's body was freckled throughout with dirty brown and white hairs intermingled.

Again, to the untrained eye the younger man's bronc might have seemed a mite scrawny, but this once wild mustang was sinewed and muscular, not to mention exceptionally sure-footed. Wilderness bred, he had the sprint of a jack rabbit and the endurance of a camel.

Al Thornton, the young rider's partner, was into his fifties and far from clean shaven. In fact his beard practically hung down to his chest and looked more like a bird's nest than facial hair. He was riding a roman-nosed bay. He carried a .45-caliber Peacemaker, like his companion. His pistol, however, was worn in a holster that was nothing more than an old, cut-down boot top that years earlier had been sewn closed at its narrow end and trimmed away at an angle at the top. Unlike the younger rider's fancy ivory-handled gun, the older man's six-shooter had plain wooden handles that were well worn from age and use.

Even though he might be older, unkempt, and grizzled, Thornton had ridden the river a time or two and seen the elephant in his day. He wasn't particularly famous, but in reality he was one of the fastest shootists west of the Mississippi.

They were both Texas Rangers.

CHAPTER ONE

Red's life had started out precariously when the wagon train his family was traveling with was attacked by a band of hostile renegade Indians. Along with the rest of the train, his parents had been killed. But, fortuitously, when the Indian attack started, the baby's mother had quickly wrapped him in a blanket and then stashed the infant in a patch of bramble bushes.

How long that infant child remained in the bushes is anyone's guess, but luckily and soon enough an old prospector was walking along with his burro and her newborn foal when he heard the baby's cries and rescued him. The child was nursed with the donkey's milk and not only survived but thrived. There was nothing that could identify the baby's family in the remains of the wagon, and since the prospector had found the red-headed baby near the Red River, he simply decided to name the boy Red.

For years thereafter the two traveled everywhere together through the Western territories. And in spite of the fact that they shared no actual familial blood, the Old Man learned to love him as if he were truly his very own son, and he took joy in watching him grow up.

The prospector taught the boy to fish and trap

and how to read sign. Red memorized every rock and gully of the West through which they roamed, a skill he was encouraged to develop by that old prospector. The Old Man also showed him how to track and hunt, and for many years the pair had very little to complain about.

It was a good life for Red and the old prospector, except for an occasional encounter with hostile Indians, the periods of drought, and times when food of any kind was scarce. Even so, the boy grew up strong and happy. He knew of no other way of living, nor did he wish for one. Life, however, like a wild river, has a nasty way of changing course when you least expect it.

When Red was fourteen years old, he and the Old Man traveled to a spot the prospector had once heard about near the southern foothills of the Rocky Mountains. After setting up camp near a small cave, the Old Man began to make a fire while the boy looked around for some kindling wood. Red climbed up an overhanging cliff and was right above the cave entrance when his foot suddenly tripped on a loose rock which in turn caused a minor rockslide.

Looking down to check on the Old Man, Red was startled to see him sprawled face down in the dirt. Fearing the worst, the boy rushed quickly to his side. When Red turned the old prospector over, he was surprised and relieved to find that not only was the man alive, but he was laughing.

What confused the boy was that the Old Man had an expression on his face that suggested what could only be described as a state of pure unbridled ecstasy.

The rockslide had opened a crack at the base of the cliff revealing what prospectors call a glory hole. In other words, it was a rocky pocket filled with nuggets of pure gold. It wasn't a vein that ran very deep or very far, but the gold found there in that hole was enough to set the old wanderer and his adopted son up for the rest of their lives.

It took the pair almost two weeks to clean out that pocket before they finally headed back to civilization. The old prospector had spent his whole life searching for such wealth and now that it was right there in his hands a sense of melancholy began to set in.

"Something wrong?" the boy asked, puzzled. "You seem more quiet than usual."

"Oh, it's nothing, Red. Just the ruminations of a tired old man."

"What's there to ruminate about?" the boy asked. "Tell me, I want to know."

The old man thought a good spell before answering. "Well, Red, it's like this. I done spent my whole life looking for just what we got in them bags. Now that I finally got it, I sort of feel. . . ." The prospector stopped and stared off into the distance.

"What?" the boy urged.

15

"Well, I don't rightly know for sure. Don't know how's to explain it to you. I expect I should still be dancing up and down for joy like I was when that hole opened up."

"But you're not," Red said, even more confused.

"Nope," the man replied, shaking his head slowly. "And that's the strange part. Maybe it wasn't the reward I was after all along. I reckon now it was the journey I enjoyed most. You know . . . the quest."

"Quest," Red repeated.

"A quest is . . . well, it's like a mission. It's the mystery and the thrill of the search all rolled into one, so to speak. Now that it's all over, I guess I'm sort of sad."

Red thought that over for a minute. "But that don't mean you can't have a new . . . what was it you called it . . . quest, does it? Maybe now that we got some money we can do new and more exciting things. Ever thought about it like that?"

The Old Man considered it as they rode along and then smiled. He seemed to perk up a bit. "Maybe you're right, Red. I never did believe it was healthy to be looking back or crying over spilt milk."

"What was it you once said to me? Every time you take a fork in the road, look on it as a new adventure. Don't be a going through life a-whining about not taking the other road or worrying about all the what-ifs."

"I said that?" The old prospector laughed. "Sounds like purty good advice."

"Sounded that way to me at the time," Red said, laughing. "So, now that we're through being all disappointed in how bad life is treating us, why don't we get back to civilization and enjoy some good food."

"Now who's the teacher and who's the pupil?" the Old Man said, chuckling as they continued on southeast.

"So how far to the town we're headed for?" the boy asked.

"I reckon we should be there in about two weeks iffen we continue on at this pace."

"Well, let's get at it then," Red replied cheerfully. "We're burning sunlight."

As they rode along over the next couple of weeks, the pair told each other all their secret desires as they pondered what having that much gold would let them do.

Red talked about getting a fine new horse and a fancy saddle. "A new hat and a pair of boots would be nice, too, don't you think?"

"You sure could use them, but no sense thinking small with this much in the poke," the Old Man remarked.

"What did you have in mind then?" Red asked.

"Well, I never was one for settling down, but right now I'm beginning to think having a nice house outside of a town might not be so bad. Nothing too fancy, but one with all the fixin's." The prospector came from a relatively well-off family, but he had chucked it all when he refused to take over his father's business. He had headed West years ago, and never looked back.

"Sure you want to plant yourself in just one spot?" the boy asked, never having known anything other than living out in the open. As long as he could remember they had never stayed in one spot long enough to even remember its name.

"Well, nothing says we still cain't take trips or wander off whenever we want," the prospector said. "Right?"

"True enough," Red replied, nodding in agreement.

Mostly out of habit, the Old Man scratched his beard. "It's just that the thought of always having some place permanent to come back to seems a mite attractive to me all of a sudden."

"Nothing wrong with having dreams, I guess," Red remarked.

"Hell's bells, Son, with this much money it don't have to be a dream no more, now does it?" The prospector was becoming more animated.

The boy smiled. "No, I guess it don't. Can you hire a person to cook for you with this much money?" he asked.

18

The Old Man laughed. " 'Course you can. But why would we do that?"

"Well, I'm the one who has had to eat your cooking all these years"—Red couldn't help but smile—"and the few times we've partaked of food in a town . . . well, it tasted gosh-darned good."

"No one puts a gun to your head at suppertime, you know," the Old Man said with a smile, but Red thought he saw hurt behind his eyes.

The back and forth banter may have become part of their daily routine, but it was all just good-natured fun to help pass the time while out on the trail.

Many days later the pair rode into Baker's Gap. It was a typical small Western town that had sprung up on the map. It was named after Eldrich Baker. A small time cowman, Baker had left the Chisum Trail halfway along and then wandered with his fifty head of cattle until he found a green valley that he thought might just suit his purpose. Eventually a town had sprung up outside his now burgeoning spread, and over the years both the ranch and the nearby town had grown and prospered pretty well.

Eldrich Baker died young, during a cattle stampede, and out of gratitude for his generosity and strong work ethic, the town elders decided to rename the place after him. Since then, it had grown to include both citizens of relatively decent morals as well as a small element of drifters and vagabonds who weren't quite so virtuous. Inevitably, a couple of saloons opened up as well as a large gambling house.

It was late in the morning when the Old Man and Red finally pulled up in front of the town bank.

"Why we stopping here?" the boy asked. "Shouldn't we drop the animals off at the livery and then find some place for the night first?"

"You forgetting what we got in them bags of ours?" the Old Man replied at a whisper. "Son, you just ain't had enough time being around citified people as you should have."

"What's that got to do with it?" Red asked. "If you're worried, we can just carry the saddlebags with us, can't we?"

"And have every passer-by wonder why two strangers who rode in with donkeys, pickaxes, and shovels are walking around with bags so heavy they's all bent over. Now that would sure enough be an invitation to a stick-up if there ever was one. Nope, the bank's gonna be our first stop. That's the smart move."

"Makes sense," Red said, pondering what he had been told. "Guess I just wasn't thinking."

"Well from now on you'll have to," the Old Man advised. "When a person has a lot of money, he has to be a step or two ahead of the other fellow who is right anxious to take it away from him."

So the pair dismounted and tied their stock up at a hitching rail located in front of the Baker's Gap Savings and Loan.

"Now you stay here with the bags till I call for you. Keep an eye on things and don't talk to no one," the Old Man ordered. "Take your rifle out of the scabbard and keep it right alongside your leg. Anything even smells suspicious, you yell out for me."

Red glanced around the town, and then looked back at the Old Man. The boy was somewhat perplexed. After all, they had just ridden for many days with the gold right where it was without a problem of any kind.

"What you worried about? Everything seems peaceful around here, don't it?" he asked.

"Out there on the trail you can see trouble a mile away," the prospector explained, pointing back the way they'd come, "but here in town things can change lickety-split. Out there no one knows your business, but in a town like this iffen you sneeze, twenty people will bless you right off, and within an hour everyone else will be asking how your nose is doing."

"I think you're worrying too much," Red said.

"Maybe so"—the Old Man nodded, knowing the boy wouldn't let anyone near the bags—"but you stay alert anyhow. This might take a bit of time."

The lad waited for about half an hour before the Old Man finally emerged from the bank.

"Come on, Red, help me get these bags offen the burro and into the bank."

When the boy entered the bank building, the first thing he noticed was a small elevated platform at the far corner of the room where a man, dressed in black, was perched in a big wooden chair. The man was staring at the front door and had on a pair of crossed pistols in a black leather holster. He also had a double-barreled shotgun lying sideways across his lap.

A bank teller came out and helped the two carry the gold through an archway and down a short hallway that led to a large iron safe. It had the thickest door the boy had ever seen and had a large metal wheel sunk right into it.

The Old Man explained: "The manager tells me they ordered this special safe door all the way from Chicagy, Illinois. Says it took them two weeks to build it in and that there ain't nothing more secure anywhere in the whole territory."

After putting the gold bags inside the safe, the pair went back out through that same steel door. Red followed the Old Man over to a section of the bank where two large desks were located. Seated at one of them was a middle-aged, balding man wearing a pair of thin-framed gold spectacles. He was dressed in a gray suit coat with a black and silver vest. Red noticed a thin gold chain hanging from the man's vest pocket, and wondered what was attached to it.

"Now then," the banker said to the Old Man, "Mister Smith, we need to have you both sign these documents before we proceed."

Red was confused. "Who's Mister Smith?" he asked, looking around to see who was behind him.

"I am," the Old Man explained. "Ain't been no reason to tell you my name all these years. It's Luke Smith, Son, and this here is Mister Jacob Reilly. He runs this place. He's going to take care of our gold."

Mr. Reilly adjusted his spectacles, pushing them up onto the bridge of his nose. "If you've never been in a bank, I can see how all this may seem strange to you, but I can assure you it is quite routine. We have discussed depositing the gold and maintaining a bank account for the two of you. So we need some documents . . . papers . . . signed by the two of you."

"An account? What's that mean exactly?" Red asked.

Mr. Reilly chuckled. "Well, you certainly can't go lugging that much gold around, so we are going to convert it to cash, according to government standards, and then we'll keep the money safely guarded here for whenever or whatever you need it for." The banker gestured toward the guard seated in the corner. "As you can see, we protect our customers' money. Besides that man, there is another guard on the roof at all times, keeping watch on the only outside door we have." He leaned over as if to whisper a secret. "And I pay another guard who is posted on a roof across the street. Anyone tries any crooked business here, he'll end up dead or in the state penitentiary quicker than you can say Davy Crockett."

"Hold our money for us, you say," Red said. "Well, what if we's in another part of the territory or maybe another town and need money? How does your keeping it all here help us?"

Jacob Reilly stifled a chuckle unsuccessfully. "Son, that's where our checks come in. They're a written promise from one bank to another bank, or even to a person or business. You just write down our information along with your information, including a private number that I will give you, and that paper will be as good as the gold you have in that safe."

Red shook his head. "A piece of paper can do all that? Just like gold?"

The Old Man nodded. "It can. Them banks all got it worked out amongst themselves, Red. See, this way we'll always have money and we won't have to worry none about getting held up out on the trail or not having enough on our persons."

"But, we always did all right for ourselves up till now, didn't we?" Red asked.

"Sure did. But we never struck it big afore. Not like this. Not enough that anyone would want to take it from us."

The bank manager nodded, adding: "Look, Son, if you are uncomfortable, well then, why don't you keep a few gold nuggets and some coins with you just in case."

Red agreed. "Sure, I guess that would be all right, being that there ain't nobody gonna argue with gold."

The two older men smiled at one another. "Right smart for a fourteen-year-old, ain't he?" the prospector remarked.

"Can I go back into that safe of yours and get me a few nuggets for my pockets like you suggested, Mister Reilly?"

"Certainly, it's your money. Just sign the paper here and here," he directed the two men.

Red hesitated before signing the paper that showed him to be "Red Smith," then he was taken back to the safe.

Once Red was gone, the Old Man leaned over the desk. "One more thing, Mister Reilly, iffen you don't mind."

The banker shook his head. "Not at all, sir. What do you need?"

The prospector reached inside his shirt and took out a piece of paper. He handed it to the bank manager. "Need you to keep this for me where it will be safe."

Mr. Reilly took the paper. "Of course. Might I ask what this is?"

"My Last Will and Testament," the Old Man

told him. "I wrote it out when I came in the bank here. I want everything split fifty-fifty, right down the middle between us, you know . . . me and the boy."

"I understand," Mr. Reilly replied.

"And if anything should happen to me, I want the boy to get it all." Pausing a moment to reflect, he then added: "I wrote down there that iffen something happens and I ain't around, he has to wait till he's twenty-five afore he can have my share. So iffen you have to take a small percentage out each year for handling the job of protecting and investing the rest of the money wisely for him, that's all right by me. Just wanna make sure Red's taken care of."

The bank manager nodded. "I understand completely."

"Also, it's so's he can't waste it all or get swindled out of it. Once he's twenty-five"— he paused a moment in thought—"well, then he can have it all to do with as he pleases. You understand?"

"Perfectly," Mr. Reilly answered. "And well thought out, I might add. I am happy to help both of you and I thank you for your confidence in our institution. I assure you, I will see to it your boy is properly protected."

Once Red returned from the safe, the pair left the bank, unhitched the horses and donkeys, and headed over to the livery stable.

CHAPTER TWO

The following morning the old prospector and the boy walked out of the two-storied hotel where they had spent the night.

"I'd almost forgot how good a clean bed and a bath can feel," the Old Man said, taking in a deep breath of fresh air.

Red yawned loudly. "The hotel bed was a little soft for my taste."

The prospector laughed. "You're just not used to it is all. Been sleeping on the ground too long. So, my boy, how about breakfast?" The lad's stomach growled. "Well, that answers that question," the Old Man observed, with a chuckle. "There's an eatery down the street that's supposed to be pretty good."

"Let's go already," Red said. "I'm so hungry my mouth is wrestling with my stomach for attention."

"Nothing some eggs and flapjacks won't cure I suspect," the Old Man said, smiling. "Having breakfast every morning is something you haven't experienced much. It's a right pleasurable custom. You'll get used to it right quick."

"Especially if you ain't the one doing the cooking," Red teased.

The old prospector feigned indignation and

tapped the boy on the head. "My cooking didn't hurt you none as far as I can see. Hell, they's full grown men what ain't so tall. And remember you got that way on my recipes."

"Like I always say," Red replied, "sometimes you get lucky, I suppose."

The two found the restaurant, a small place with a large front window and a sign that said: *Edith's Eatery*. They entered and found a table just off to the right of the door.

After a moment or two, a rather heavy-set lady came out from the back. Her graying hair was in a bun at the nape of her neck and she wore a blue floral dress and an apron with white lacing on the edges.

"Good morning, gentlemen. My name is Edith and I'll be more than happy to serve you." The pair had cleaned up at the hotel, but considering that they hadn't had time to do any shopping and were still wearing their tattered trail clothes, calling them *gentlemen* seemed rather generous. "Can I start you off with some coffee?" she asked.

"You're in town now, boy," the Old Man reminded him, "so remember to say please, especially to such an attractive lady." *The Old Man must have had his share of sweethearts in his younger days back East,* the boy thought as Edith laughed.

She tapped the Old Man on the shoulder.

"Oh, go on now. And me at my age. I do swear."

The Old Man shook his head. "Don't talk like that. True beauty is timeless."

Red squirmed and cleared his throat. "You gonna order, or am I gonna have to die of hunger here while you two jibber-jabber. I'd like eggs and flapjacks . . . and plenty of bacon."

Edith smiled. "We've got bacon a-plenty. All you can eat."

"Might as well kill an extra hog then, ma'am, 'cause I ain't had restaurant cooking in a heap of time," Red said.

All three laughed at this.

"And for you, sir?" Edith asked.

The prospector thought a moment. "Flapjacks with a mountain of butter and three . . . no, four eggs, sunny-side down."

"Coming right up." As she walked away the two could hear her chuckle. "Attractive? Hmm."

The meal was every bit as good as promised and the two took their sweet time savoring every bite. When they were finished, the boy looked up from his plate and asked: "So what are the plans for the day?"

The Old Man reached into his pocket and took out a few of the coins that he had gotten at the bank and placed them on the table. "I reckon we'll get some new clothes, a haircut, and then we can go find out if there's any ranches for sale around here. Sound good to you, boy?"

Red nodded in agreement. "And some new boots."

Edith smiled at the pair when they rose from the table. As they were leaving, Red couldn't help but notice that she winked at the prospector. *Maybe he ain't as old as I figured,* the boy thought to himself.

"Keep eating like this and I'm gonna need a bigger belt before long," the prospector said, patting his belly.

"That be so bad?" Red asked.

The Old Man thought a moment and grinned. "No, I don't reckon it would. Might just be I'll end up enjoying this here new found life of leisure."

The pair headed across the street toward a general sundries store they had noticed when they first rode into town. They were about half-way down the street when loud yelling and a shot rang out off to their right. Suddenly the bat-wing doors of the gambling house burst open and two men ran out.

A loud yell came from inside the place. "Some-one stop those two! We've been robbed by those cheaters!"

Red stopped, fascinated by what he was seeing. He had heard about shoot-outs and walk-downs but he had never witnessed one.

A man suddenly came rushing past between them, yelling: "Out of the way! Get down!" As the man pulled his gun, his vest fell open and Red saw the badge. The lawman shouted: "Hold it right there! I said stop in the name of the law!"

The two outlaws had just reached a pair of horses tethered down the street. Then they both stopped, turned, and started firing their guns. There wasn't a moment of hesitation from either one of them.

The sheriff spun around and fell to the ground with blood spilling from his left shoulder. Before anyone could do anything to prevent it, the two men mounted their horses and rode out of town, firing a few random shots to keep everyone back.

"Did you see that!" Red exclaimed to the Old Man, who was behind him. "The man, he . . ." The boy stopped short. There, face down on the ground, was the man who for the last fourteen years had raised him, protected him, and loved him like a father truly loves a son.

Red dropped to his knees and turned the Old Man over. Blood had already begun seeping through his shirt. His eyes were lifeless. A bullet meant for the sheriff had hit him instead was all Red could think.

"No, no, no, no, no!" the boy screamed. "Somebody do something! Please do something!"

By this time people were gathering around the old fellow and the sheriff. One of the men put an arm on Red's shoulder as he felt for a pulse on the old prospector, saying to Red: "Sorry, boy, but it looks like he's gone."

Then someone called out: "Quick! Someone go tell Doc Burns to be ready while a couple of you men help me carry the sheriff over to his house."

"But the two killers, they're getting away," Red sobbed.

"Son, they's already got away, the dirty swines," a bearded fellow told him as he bent over to help Red stand, which he refused to do. Shaking his head, the man added: "By the time we get the sheriff here patched up and try to gather up a posse, well, let's face it, they'll be long gone from here."

"Who were they? Anyone know?" Red asked, looking desperately into the faces of those who remained.

A few of the men shook their heads, but one finally replied: "New to town. Just a pair of cardsharp crooks, I guess. Not very good though. They got caught bottom dealing and that's when the ruckus started. Took our money at gunpoint."

"But isn't anyone going to do anything?" Red asked.

"Nothing to do, son," the bearded fellow said. "Not now anyway, except maybe try to help the sheriff here. Got to worry about the living ones first."

Red took one last look at the Old Man's lifeless body, and in that instant he ceased being a boy.

A fury arose deep within him such as he had never known. He stood up, wiped his tears on his sleeve, and quickly searched the plank walks for a specific sign. Then he found it. Painted in white block letters in the window of a store about a half a block away was the sign he was looking for. It read: *Ed Farrell, Gunsmith.*

The boy pushed through the crowd and made a quick beeline straight for the shop. He practically took the door off its hinges as he barged in.

"Hey, what is this? Easy there, pardner," the smithy said firmly.

"I want the best pistol you have, two boxes of bullets for it, and the newest and best long rifle you have."

The gunsmith took one look at the sight before him and laughed out loud. He didn't expect a boy the likes of him, wearing a hat with part of its brim torn, to be a potential customer. He shook his head at the thought of it.

"Right, and I want to marry Lillie Langtry, but that ain't happening, either. Now go away, boy, and on your way out close the door gently this time."

His anger growing, Red walked up to the counter and glared at the man. He reached into his pocket and pulled out a large gold nugget. Ed Farrell's eyes practically popped out of his head when he saw the size of it. "Mister, you don't know me and I don't know you, but my Pa and

I just rode into town after striking it rich. He just got shot down. You heard the shooting I expect."

"Yes, I did," the gunsmith said, recalling how he had run to the back room at the time.

Red stared hard at the man. "Listen, if you don't believe this is real gold, you can check with the banker. But by that time, I'll have taken what I want, one way or another. Or you can take this whole gold nugget here, give me what I asked for, and then we'll both be satisfied."

The gunsmith knew he was looking at enough gold to equal at least six months' worth of hard work, so he quickly changed his attitude.

"Best pistol in the place, huh? Well, sir, that'd be this new Colt Forty-Five here, a Peacemaker. Smoothest action I ever saw, and these grips here are ivory for a better hold when yer hands is wet or slippery," Farrell explained as he extended the pistol over the counter.

After examining it, Red had to admit that just holding it in his hands seemed special.

"I'll throw in two full boxes of Forty-Five-caliber bullets," the gunsmith added.

"What about that rifle I mentioned?" Red reminded the man. "I want the best and surest one in the store, and I swear if you try to cheat me, I'll be back. . . ."

Ed Farrell got a little angry himself. "Look, kid, like you said, I don't know who you are and you don't know me, but you go and ask anyone around here. They'll tell you if you do business in my shop, every gun I sell will work like a Swiss clock and shoot straight. If you don't hit nothing, it's your fault, not the gun's."

"I'm in a hurry, mister," Red said impatiently. "The rifle?"

The gunsmith looked over at his rack of rifles, and after a moment's hesitation pulled down a lever-action Winchester.

"This one's a Thirty-Thirty, so it has a bit of a kick," he informed Red. "But I don't imagine that'll be a problem for a big lad like yourself. It's brand new and the action is as sweet as my wife's pecan pie."

"Why is this barrel shorter than those others?" Red asked, studying the guns lined up on the rack.

"It's a carbine model," he said. "I'll admit it's a mite shorter, but the firepower is still the same. The way I figure it, this model should fit your shoulder and arm reach better. Trust me on this one. After twenty years at it, I know what I'm talking about when it comes to matching guns with men. It comes with that sling thrown in."

Satisfied, Red nodded in agreement. "Fine, and I'll need two boxes of Thirty-Thirty bullets."

The man placed two boxes on the counter. "I don't have a holster right now that will fit your waist size, but if you come back tomorrow, I can have one cut down and ready for you by then."

"Thanks, but no time for that," Red said. After loading the Colt pistol, he stuck it through his belt and then tapped the nugget with his finger. "We good here?"

The man stared at the boy and nodded. "For some reason I don't expect I'm doing you any favors, but I'm not going to waste time arguing with a stubborn *hombre* like you. And yes, we are more than good here." The gunsmith slid the gold nugget off the counter and quickly dropped it in his vest pocket.

"Thanks. And rest assured, it's a favor you're doing me," Red said, as he loaded the rifle and slung it over his left shoulder. Then, grabbing up the boxes, he hurried out of the shop.

Once outside, Red quickly got his bearings and then ran to the livery stable.

The liveryman was using a pitchfork to clean up the loose straw around the outside corral when Red approached. He saw the pistol and the rifle and quickly sized up the situation.

"Already heard the shots and heard about the old fellow that rode in with you. Your kin?"

Impatient to get on the trail, Red merely dipped his head in a singular nod, saying: "Which is the fastest and strongest horse in the stable? And how much?"

The liveryman stroked his beard and replied: "That'd be the chocolate roan back in the far stall. He's still a mite young, but he's strong as an ox, faster than a jack rabbit, and sure-footed as a mountain goat. But he's not for sale."

"Why not?" Red asked angrily.

"Well, for one thing he's my own horse," the man replied. "Raised him from a foal."

"Mister, I was once told that everything has a price," Red stated firmly, looking the liveryman in the eye.

"Well, that may be true," the man agreed, "but I doubt you'd be able to afford what I'd have to ask for him."

When the boy pulled out a large gold nugget from his pocket the man's eyes reacted just as those of the gunsmith's had.

"Well, even iffen I would sell him," the man said, stroking his chin, "and I ain't saying I will, I could never make change for that." His eyes never left the hand holding the gold.

Red shook his head. "You don't understand. This whole nugget is yours. I just need the horse, a good saddle, and a canteen of water."

It took all of a whole two seconds for the liveryman to decide. "It's a deal. When you need him by?"

"Right away. I'm going to get my own horse ready . . . the sorrel gelding I rode in on. Hurry and don't forget that canteen of water, and make sure you put a good saddle and blanket on him."

"Right away, son, and for that much gold I'll give you my own saddle, too. Got it in San

Antonio. Tooled leather. Ain't none prettier."

"That sounds good, but, mister, you better not cheat me in any way, or I'll be back to collect," he said, tapping his new Colt revolver."

The man laughed at the boy's brashness, but for some reason he didn't doubt the lad for one moment. Besides, with the firepower the boy was carrying, he wasn't about to argue with him. "One roan with a good sound saddle on him coming right up."

Twenty minutes later, the liveryman stood outside, watching as the all fired-up teenager in tattered clothes galloped out on his sorrel gelding, the reins of the big chocolate roan in his hand.

"Revenge sure as shootin' if I ever saw it," the man said to himself sadly. He reached into his pocket, felt for the gold nugget, and slowly shook his head. "I wish you luck, boy. It was only fer a short time, but even so, I kinda liked your old man when I met him."

CHAPTER THREE

There was no doubt that the events of three days earlier had stirred up a lot of conversation and speculation among the townsfolk of Baker's Gap.

By now, in a town of this size, almost everyone had heard of the shoot-out and the old prospector's death. They also heard stories from both the gunsmith and the liveryman, although both conveniently left out the part about being overpaid with the boy's gold nuggets. Only the banker knew those details, and he was known to be a very tight-lipped gentleman.

Although no one in town really knew the old prospector or the boy, everyone assumed they were father and son and that the boy had recklessly ridden out in a state of anger seeking the two men who had murdered his father.

There were some—mostly women—who said that Ed Farrell, the gunsmith, was blinded by his greed, and that if anything bad should happen to the boy, which it surely would, he would be responsible. His only defense was that the boy was so insistent, there was simply no arguing with him.

Bob Dickens, the liveryman, offered a similar explanation. "A stubborn kid like that?" he'd reply. "Already armed with a rifle and pistol? I'm a-telling you, there was just no arguing with him. Besides, he was willing to pay a fair price."

Seeing as how Dickens had a reputation for being a miser, no one believed for a minute that he had settled on a *fair* price for his own horse.

There was little doubt among the townsfolk that the boy would meet his end out on the trail. They were relieved to hear that Sheriff Tom Harrison was recuperating from his shoulder wound, and that Doc Burns believed he would make a full recovery. Harrison had been town marshal for five years and had never had a setback like this. In fact, once Doc had dug the bullet out, the sheriff had tried to go after the murderers more than once, but he was too weak as it had taken some effort on the part of Doc Burns to dig out the bullet.

Prior to this event, Baker's Gap had been a relatively peaceful town. Tom had efficiently seen to that on more than one occasion. He was a widower, his wife and son having been killed years earlier in a Comanche raid. He had been away, driving cattle, and had never forgiven himself for what had happened to them. Even though he knew nothing of Red or the man who had been killed, he was worried about the boy. Riding out after outlaws was his job, but with his arm in a sling and Doc Burns insisting that he stay put, there was little he could do but stew and curse himself.

"I walked right into it, Doc. The fastest gun in the county and still I get shot. Took one like a tenderfoot," the lawman said, shaking his head in disgust. At the time, he was getting his bandage changed in the Burns's home where Doc carried out his practice.

The doctor shook his head and set his scissors down on the table next to him. "Listen to me good, Tom. You walked right into something unexpected. Hell, it went off so fast you couldn't have even known what was going on or who was doing what. You can't blame yourself, Tom, no one else does."

"Yeah? Well, tell that to the boy and the old prospector. Oh, right, you can't. The man's dead and the boy's long gone. I'm the sheriff. I'm supposed to react quickly and precisely in situations like this. It's what they pay me for."

Doc Burns adjusted his spectacles. "And they will go on paying you. Look here, Tom, there isn't a man or woman who doesn't know that you didn't hesitate at the first sign of trouble. You put yourself right in the midst of the danger."

"Right into the firing line." Tom Harrison was almost tearing up, but it wasn't from the pain. "Hell of a lot of good it did the old man. Or the boy for that matter. Doc, that young 'un is out there all alone. If he's not dead already that is. What chance does a boy that age have against two fully grown stone-cold killers?"

"Oh, I'll agree he doesn't have much of a chance against those two," the doctor said, shaking his head sadly. "But remember back to when you were his age. How many times have you told me that you were punching cattle for Dan Steel's outfit at fifteen?" The sheriff shrugged while the doctor began easing the sheriff's arm back in the shoulder sling he had fashioned. "And besides, maybe it'll work out and he'll lose their trail. You just wait, that boy will probably come limping back in here without even a scratch on him, hungry as a bear coming out of hibernation."

"I hope so. It just galls me that I didn't help him is all."

"You're alive, Tom. Stop worrying about things and you'll have a full recovery, if you listen to my advice. You should be grateful it wasn't worse."

"Thanks, Doc. It's just that I keep thinking the kid is about the same age as my boy Johnny would have been . . . if he'd lived. If anything happens to that boy, it'll be like going through it all over again. And I can't help thinking it would be my fault."

"Nonsense. Any blame rests totally on those two outlaws. You can't be responsible for a vengeful boy's stubborn streak. You mustn't let it tear you apart."

The doc had barely gotten the words out when there was a shout from the street just outside the

42

house. The two inside could see people running along the plank walkway, but they couldn't see what they were looking at because they had stopped and were blocking the view out to the street.

"Now what?" muttered the sheriff, as he wrenched himself away. He reached down to his holster with his good arm and pulled out his Remington single-action revolver.

Doc Burns looked down at the gun and then up at the face of his friend.

Harrison shook his head. "Not again, Doc. You won't catch me daydreaming this time."

"Be careful Tom. We don't know yet what's happening."

The two men went to the door, and when the doctor yanked it open the sheriff stepped quickly out into the street, his hand by his holster. The doctor followed closely behind.

Riding slowly and steadily down the street was a lanky boy in tattered clothes and a torn hat on a chocolate roan horse and trailing two chestnut horses. A dead body was draped over the saddle on each of the chestnuts.

With a group of children running behind him, Red rode straight for the sheriff's office. He dismounted slowly, arching his back to relieve the stiffness before he walked up to the door. It was locked.

He turned when a loud voice shouted out at him: "Wait a minute and I'll open it for you! Get back," he snapped at the people who were following him. Tom Harrison took a key out of his pocket and unlocked the door to his office. "You there, Bill and Harry," the sheriff ordered, "take the bodies over to the undertaker, and get those chestnuts over to Dickens at the livery. I'll be along as soon as I can."

Turning to Red, he said softly: "Come on in, boy, and tell me what happened."

"I'd appreciate some water first," Red rasped. "I'm kinda parched."

"Sure, son." The sheriff took a cup down off a wooden wall peg and poured some water from a large pitcher that he kept on a small side table.

"What's your name, boy?" he asked.

"I'm called Red. I was named after the river."

"Well, just take your time, Red. You're among friends here. Just tell me what happened when you're ready, so I can make up a report."

The boy started gulping the water like there was no tomorrow.

"Go easy there," Sheriff Harrison warned as he sat down, indicating to the boy that there was plenty more water. Red emptied a second cup, then took a chair in front of the desk.

"Now then, tell me, was that your pa that got killed?"

Red set the empty cup down and nodded. "Next

closest thing. Found me out on the trail as a cub and raised me all these years. All the kin I ever known. Just found out his name was Luke Smith. Always called him Old Man . . . sometimes Pa. He found me when I was just a baby. The wagon train was attacked . . . everybody killed but me."

Harrison shook his head. "So there's no one else to care for you?"

The lad looked up defiantly. "I don't need no one to take care of me. I can take care of myself." He looked out the window, forgetting the dead men and the horses had been ushered away. "Guess I proved that, didn't I?"

"Sort of looks that way," the sheriff agreed. "Didn't mean for you to take offense. Everybody needs someone around. Friends and such. 'Less they're a hermit. Are you a hermit, boy?"

Red wanted to lash out at the sheriff, but it seemed this man, this stranger, was genuinely concerned about him. "I'm not a hermit. It's just that it was always the two of us out there. We did fine for ourselves. The Old Man taught me to read and write, to track, shoot, and hunt. He taught me something everywhere we traveled. Hell, he even taught me to speak Kiowa."

That last remark surprised the sheriff, who for good reason had little use for the native population.

"All right, so what exactly happened out there? I mean after you rode out of town," Tom said.

"I used an old Indian trick the Old Man taught me. I rode my sorrel until it couldn't go no farther, then switched to the roan, it being the stronger mount. That's why I could catch up so quickly, what with them just having the one horse apiece. I knew they were pushing their animals hard when they first rode out of town, and that they'd have to rest 'em or at least walk 'em from time to time to keep 'em from tiring out. And I didn't."

Tom Harrison sat, nodding. "Mexican *vaqueros* do that, but they actually jump from one horse to the other at a full-out run. Call it *el paso de la muerte*. Means the leap of death. Did you know that?"

"Comanches and Kiowa do it, too," Red told him. "After a day or so I could tell where they was headed. The Old Man once told me that trailing something or someone isn't just about reading their tracks, but about thinking like the prey does."

"That's what good lawmen do," Harrison said. "I learned the same thing."

"They weren't real careful about covering their tracks," Red continued. "Knew what they needed . . . water for themselves and their horses, food, and sleep. I figured they wasn't going to stick anywhere around here, seeing as how they shot a sheriff and murdered someone." He paused, catching his breath on that last sentence.

"Take your time, Red," the sheriff said patiently.

"Well, sir, I knew which way they was heading from the tracks they was making. There was only one way they could go that would get them out of the area, but still provide the water they'd need along the way. Knowing that, it was just a matter of getting out in front of them. That part was easy. Like I said before, know the land around here like the back of my hand."

Tom Harrison marveled at how mature and trail-wise the boy was. He began to feel almost a sense of pride in the kid. "But there were two of them and you're just . . ."

Red glared at him.

The lawman hesitated. "You're just one person."

"I am. So I wasn't about to give them any more of a chance than they done the Old Man . . ."—he glanced at Harrison's shoulder—"and you."

Red's acknowledgment of Harrison's injury made the lawman uncomfortable, but he bobbed his head and urged Red to go on.

"I rode out ahead of them and then waited in this rocky outcrop. When they appeared, I made sure they was the right fellows. I recognized them, all right."

"But you only got a glimpse of them. And it all happened in a matter of a minute or so," the sheriff said.

"I learned a long time ago you better notice

things right off. Might mean the difference between life and death."

Tom smiled. "Well, you got me there. I agree. Said the same thing a time or two myself. Just thought that someone so . . ." He caught himself before bringing up the boy's youth again. "Never mind."

The boy reached over and poured some more water but just took a couple of sips this time. When he was finished, he wiped his mouth with his sleeve and continued his story.

"Like I was saying, I hid in that outcrop until they both rode past. Then I shot one of them off his horse. Got the man right in the chest. He was dead before he hit the ground. I used my own single-shot rifle for that one 'cause I've had more practice with it. Trust it more."

"The other fellow make a run for it?" the sheriff asked. His curiosity had gotten the better of him.

"No, sir. He pulled his rifle out and dropped off his mount. Then he took cover amongst some nearby boulders. Didn't even bother to check on his partner, the louse," the boy commented. "When he started shooting at me, I returned fire right back at him, but I took my own sweet time reloading so's he'd know it was only a single-shot rifle I was using."

"Why'd you do that?" Tom asked.

"So that when I dropped it, he'd figure he had the upper hand."

"You dropped your rifle on purpose? Good grief!" Sheriff Harrison couldn't believe what he was hearing, but he had to smile at the boy's gumption.

Red nodded. "Yep. Fumbled it right on over the rocks. Then I got up, leaned over, and yelled like it was the dumbest accident in the world. Well, sir, next I started taking shots back at him one at a time with my new pistol. Pretty quickly that fellow realized I only had a six-shooter pistol. Guess he reckoned I couldn't match his rifle for range. After a while I heard him laugh and yell a few curses up at me. Then I heard him heading up the rocks to get me."

It was only then that Sheriff Harrison remembered the gunsmith mentioning that he had also sold the boy a Winchester carbine. When he realized what kind of cold calculation such actions implied, he looked at the boy with both wonder and respect.

"He walked right in range of you and your carbine, didn't he." Harrison said it more as a statement than a question.

Red said nothing.

The sheriff realized that he had been so caught up in the boy's story that he hadn't remembered to take notes. But that didn't worry him. Tom Harrison wasn't likely to forget what he had just been told.

CHAPTER FOUR

The sheriff went off to see the undertaker and meet with Dickens at the livery, leaving Red alone in his office. When Harrison returned, he made a pot of coffee before he announced: "I don't think you should leave Baker's Gap for a while. You can stay with me."

Red shook his head. "Don't seem likely I have a reason to do that."

"I think you do," Harrison began, trying to lure the boy in. "You've no place to go and no one to go with. I, on the other hand, have a good-size house and could use some help keeping the place up, especially now with this bum shoulder of mine. You'd be doing me a favor of sorts. Besides, we could sort of keep each other company, if you don't mind my boring conversation too much."

"Don't even know you," the boy remarked.

"One way to get acquainted, ain't it?" Tom smiled.

"I suppose," Red mumbled.

"And now that things are back to normal in town, I can help you find whatever things you might be needing." He looked at the threadbare cuffs and elbows of Red's shirt. "New clothes or anything else you might need. Might even be a help in deciding what you're going to do next.

Come on, give it a few days and let's see how it goes. I might not be the best cook in town, but my house has got plenty of room. Even have an extra bed. Now's not a good time for you to be alone."

Red couldn't argue with the man's reasoning. He nodded his agreement, but after a moment's thought said: "I need to see the Old Man first. You know . . . make sure he's taken care of proper."

Tom got up and put his hand on the boy's shoulder. "Son, this town didn't get off to a very good start with you, but believe me when I tell you it's full of good people who sincerely regret what happened to your pa. While you were gone, they arranged to have him buried in our cemetery real nice, with a minister saying the words and all."

"I'd like to go there and pay my respects first thing," Red stated.

"No problem. We waited on putting up a marker. We didn't know if you'd ever be back, but we hoped you would and so we decided to wait. Figured you'd want to make the decision about it yourself, it being a personal matter. You sure you don't want to get something to eat before we go over there?"

Red shook his head. "No. Want to pay my respects first. I owe the Old Man a lot more than that."

After locking the office, he and Red rode out of town and up the hill north of town.

There was a tall ornate archway framing the entrance to the cemetery, with a sign on top that read: *Baker's Gap Necropolis.* Red smiled as he read the words carved into a large stone that was near the entrance. *Most everyone who stays here is equal in the eyes of the Lord.*

The Old Man had never expressed any particular notions about religion or the afterlife, or even how he wanted to be remembered. Red had never given it a passing thought, figuring they would always be together. But now, looking around at the rows of graves, some with headstones, most with wooden crosses, all lined up, he felt this was as good a place as any for his pa's final resting place.

"Over there . . . under that big tree," the sheriff said, and pointed out the plot. "I'll leave you alone with him to say good bye."

Red walked slowly over to the freshly covered grave site, reflecting on how the mound reminded him of all their gold digging together over the years. Stopping at the grave, tears welled up in his eyes and he smiled sadly. "You always was digging up holes, Pa, all over the place," he began. "Guess this is your last one. I expect iffen there's a place up there for good folks to go to rest in peace, they'll let you in without nary a question. I want to thank you for all you done, and don't you be worrying none about me. I'll be all right. I even got it in my mind what I'd like to do with my life. It likely won't involve any more picks and shovels, but it should be useful just the same. If I do it right."

Tom Harrison watched the boy at a respectful distance, waiting for him to return so they could head back to town.

"We're going to get something to eat now, Red, whether you're hungry or not," Harrison said as they rode back into Baker's Gap. "I know I sure as hell am. We still have some things to discuss, and then the next thing on the agenda will be to get you fitted out with some new clothes."

"And a new hat and boots," Red added enthusiastically.

Tom smiled. "Right, but first on the list is vittles. Come on, follow me."

The sheriff said the best eatery in town was Edith's, the same place the Old Man and Red had gone. Upon entering, Tom took off his hat and hung it on a coat rack. Red did the same.

"Hello, Edith. There's two of us," the sheriff said when the owner peeked out from the back.

Drying her hands, she came out and looked at the boy a moment before recognizing him, then tears came to her eyes. "Oh, you poor thing," she whispered, and wrapped Red up in big arms. "How horrible it must be for you. Lordy mercy." Then Edith released the embarrassed boy and escorted the two to a nearby table. "What happened to that kind man is an outrage. You just sit right here and I'll fix you both up something special."

The pair sat down, and when Red looked around the room he could see people staring at him. "I'm not used to this much attention," he whispered to the lawman.

"Well, it isn't every day that someone so young brings in two killers all by his lonesome. I expect they're just curious is all. It'll wear off once they get to know you."

"Don't plan on them getting to know me," he replied suspiciously as he glanced around the room again.

Red wiped his face on his sleeve before putting his elbows up on the table as if to signal he was ready to eat.

"Miss Edith runs a respectable place here, so remember your etiquette," Tom said, frowning.

"What's eh-ti-kit?" Red asked, unsure of what he had done wrong.

"It's the difference between stable manners and table manners," the sheriff told him with a smile. "So elbows off the table."

It wasn't long before Edith appeared with two bowls of hot soup and a pyramid of sourdough biscuits. "This'll start you off, but take your time, there's more coming up."

Over their meal the two discussed the immediate future.

"Have you thought any about what you want to put on a marker for your pa? If you decide on a stone marker, it'll take some time to get it here and have it carved."

"I don't even know what goes on a marker. But I think the Old Man might like something simple, a plain wooden one," the boy said.

Tom ignored Red's last comment. "Well, what one usually puts on a headstone is the person's name and his birthdate and his date of death. Maybe a saying of some kind . . ."

"Like what?" Red broke in.

Tom thought a moment. "Oh, you know, things like . . . maybe 'Rest in peace' or 'Beloved father.' Whatever you like."

Red remained silent as he thought over the idea. "I don't even know when he was born, but if I was to put up a headstone, I would want it to say Bear Slayer."

"Did you say Bear Slayer?" Tom said, his brow furrowing.

Red nodded. "Yep. I think he'd like that."

"That's kinda unusual," the lawman said. "Do you mind telling me why you'd think he'd like that? Not prying, just trying to understand is all."

"It's the name the Kiowas gave him when he was young man," Red explained. "Bear Slayer is a translation, or at least close to it."

"And just how did he get that name? I mean aside from the obvious one."

Red chuckled before he answered the sheriff. "Well, it was one of his favorite stories to tell me." Red closed his eyes and tried to think of the way the Old Man told it. He wanted to honor the story and tell it just like the Old Man had so many times to him.

"Well, it's like this," he began. "Many years ago when he was a young man, he was prospecting up north and west of the Panhandle when suddenly he heard a horrible noise coming from the far side of a large stand of trees. He tied up his mule, mounted his horse, and pulled his Fifty-caliber Hawkins rifle out. He rode through the trees to the other side of the grove where he saw a young Indian brave being attacked by a large black bear. There were about ten others in the group with him, but when the bear charged, they must've scattered. The Old Man figured he had to act since he couldn't just stand there and watch the bear maul that Indian."

"So what'd he do?" Tom asked, taking the story in with a grain of salt.

"Well, sir, I'll tell you," Red said, happy to see that the sheriff was as interested in the story as he had always been. "He spurred his mount and attacked that bear on horseback. As he charged, he fired that Hawkins, and when he got closer, he pulled his single-shot flintlock belt gun and fired it, too. Problem was that the two shots just got the bear all riled up. Took its attention away from the Indian it was attacking though." Red stopped to laugh just as the Old Man always did at this point.

"He wouldn't have had time to reload," Tom pointed out. "Not back then. Those single-shot muskets were deadly, but nowhere near as fast as an angry bear."

"You're right. So the Old Man got out his hunting knife and just rode that horse up to the bear as fast as he could. Then he leaped out of his saddle and onto the bear's back with the knife in his hand."

"I don't believe it," Tom said dismissively.

"Oh, you can believe it," Red assured him. "Many is the time I saw his scars from that fight. Ain't nothing makes marks like that 'cepting a bear claw. Anyway, he dove onto that bear's back and began stabbing it for dear life. His not the bear's." Red smiled as he remembered how the Old Man had always liked to tell the particulars of the story. "Finally, when the fur stopped flying, both the Old Man and the bear was lying on the ground, only the bear wasn't breathing no more."

"What'd the Indians do?" Tom asked.

"As it turned out the man was a Kiowa war chief, and him and his hunting party was hunting far north of their usual stomping grounds. Maybe game was scarce that year, I don't know. At any rate both the Indian and the Old Man were tore up something awful. So the others in the party patched them up as best they could, and they skinned and butchered the bear." Red paused to take a drink of the coffee Edith had brought them. "Well, sir, that band went back south and took him right along with them. They continued to care for him until he was healed up. Them Kiowas honored him for saving their chief by giving him a necklace they had made with some of the bear claws on it."

"You said the Kiowas gave him that name, didn't you?" Tom asked.

Red nodded. "He stayed on and lived with them for a couple of years more before he finally got the itch to move on. One day he just up and left and went back to prospecting."

"That's too tall a tale even for me," the sheriff said in total disbelief.

"Believe it," Red said, and unbuttoned the top of his shirt, reached in, and pulled out a necklace with three bear claws strung together with beads. The claws were among the largest ones Tom Harrison had ever seen.

"Bear Slayer it is then," Tom said, smiling and shaking his head. "Guess all that's left is for you to decide what kind of marker you want," he said.

When they were finished with the chicken dinner Edith had served, the lawman pushed back his chair and rose from the table. He stood there for a time, looking at Red before he finally spoke.

"So it's agreed. For now you're staying with me. In the morning we'll go see Jacob Reilly over at the bank since you said you have business there, and then we'll get you fitted out with some new clothes . . . boots and hat included. After that we can talk about what comes next."

Red yawned loudly. "I also want to make sure the roan is taken care of over at the livery. I got to liking him right quick."

Sheriff Harrison looked down at the boy. "Yeah, sometimes it happens like that."

CHAPTER FIVE

The next morning, when they were finished eating a breakfast of eggs, bacon, and hot buttered biscuits, Red leaned back, patted his stomach, and said: "I haven't eaten regular like this in . . . well, never. I thought you said you weren't that good a cook."

The lawman laughed. "Tell you a little secret. Since I'm a widower, the women around here drop food off for me every so often. Trying to get on my good side, I guess. But when they got wind of how you were staying here, they cooked up enough food and brought in enough vegetables and other supplies to last us at least a week. There's a stew for dinner right over there."

"Widower? You was married?" Red asked.

"Yeah I was married," he affirmed, a wistful look passing over his face. "Lost my wife and son about ten years back to Comanches. We had a ranch a couple of hundred miles west of here. The boy was only four at the time. Both were way too young to die. Annabelle was prettier than a man like me could ever dream of marrying. Good woman, good mother, and a great wife."

"Sorry," Red said sincerely.

"Long time ago," Tom reflected. "So you see, you're doing me a favor by staying on. Help keep me company, and who knows . . . maybe the food'll keep a comin'."

Red said nothing. He was still noncommittal, never having lived in a town.

As they started to leave the house, the boy grabbed up his pistol and stuck it in his belt.

"You won't need that with me along," the sheriff said confidently.

Red pointed at the man's sling. "No offense, but I don't believe that's necessarily true." When he saw the expression on the sheriff's face, Red immediately regretted his comment. "Sorry, that was uncalled for."

"Forget it. But I repeat . . . you won't need that."

"Again no offense, Sheriff, but I've been sleeping with a firearm within reach since I was knee-high to a possum."

"Out on the trail sure, but we're in town now," Harrison reminded him.

"And nothing bad ever happens in town? We heard that this was a nice peaceful place and less than a day after arriving the Old Man gets killed. I think I'll just carry this with me, anyway."

"You are a stubborn one, aren't you?" Tom said, shaking his head.

The pair ended up criss-crossing the town all morning, from livery to the general store, from the leather smith to the town barber. They put off going to the undertaker to discuss a marker, but thcy did go to the bank. As Red walked through the bank door, he kept looking down at his new boots with pride.

Jacob Reilly was pleased to see the two entering his establishment. He stood up and extended a hand to the sheriff. "Glad to see you up and around, Tom." The man hesitated a moment before gesturing toward the chairs in front of his desk.

"As for you, son, I am real sorry about your father."

"Yes, sir, and thank you," Red said, taking a seat. The sheriff sat down next to him.

"I wanted to talk to you about the gold we left here in the bank," Red said, jumping right in. "I'm sort of trying to figure out what to do next."

The banker nodded as he sat down. "I am sure it all seems overwhelming. Please, let me explain." He opened a drawer in his desk and took out an envelope and then unfolded the sheet of paper inside. "Have you seen this?" he asked Red. "Do you know what this is?"

Red looked at the paper and shook his head. "No, sir. Never saw it before."

"Well, this is your pa's Last Will and Testament. Wrote right here in this bank. So let me explain it in simple terms. This is a legal document your pa wrote to outline what the bank was supposed to do in the event of his . . . um . . . passing."

Red looked at the sheriff and back at Reilly. "And?"

The banker looked over at the sheriff and smiled. "Well, simply put, with your portion of the gold that you two discovered you would be considered well-to-do for the rest of your life. However, with your pa's passing"—he tapped the paper—"his half of the gold is to be transferred to you when you are a little older. Twenty-five to be exact. Except, that is, for a small amount to be used by the bank for managing your accounts and insuring your capital."

"So what does that all mean exactly?"

Jacob Reilly let out a small laugh. "Son, it means that you are a very wealthy young man. Very wealthy, indeed."

Reilly looked at the sheriff. "I'm going to give the sheriff here this copy of the will so the two of you can go over it and confirm that what I have told you are the wishes of your pa as expressed in the document. I have already transferred your pa's share of the funds into a private account. It will accrue interest until you are twenty-five. In the meantime, your account will always have more than enough money in it to meet your needs and then some. I must say, few of your age, or any age, can even dream of being in your position."

Red thought of all the good years he had spent with the Old Man. "Somehow I don't feel much like being in this position right now," he said softly.

The banker nodded his head. "And that is totally understandable. But believe me, son, I promised Mister Smith, your pa, that I would watch out for your best interests and I don't give my word lightly. Just ask Tom here if you have any doubts."

The sheriff nodded. "I would stake all I have on Jacob's word. I think anyone in town will tell you the same."

Red looked from Tom to the banker. "I want some money now, so I can pay for all the things I bought and pay the sheriff here for all his help."

"Not a problem, my boy. It'll take just a moment." Jacob Reilly headed for the closest teller.

Tom shook his head. "Red, you don't owe me a thing."

"That's not the way I see it," Red replied.

"Tell you what," Harrison said. "Let's go back home. I think I may have a proposal you just might like."

The banker came back and, after counting out the money, he handed it to Red. The sheriff stared incredulously.

"That's more than I make in months," he commented, scratching his head.

"Which is precisely why it's important that someone trustworthy protect this boy's interests," the banker reaffirmed.

Red became angered and patted the revolver stuck in his belt. "Stop calling me a boy. I can take care of myself."

"I'm sure you can," Reilly said, flinching slightly in his chair. "But that's with things you know about. I'm talking about con artists, crooked gamblers, and people looking for investors. Ever heard of a bunco artist, a sting, or a blackmail set-up?"

"No, sir," Red replied truthfully.

"Let me help with this, Jacob," Tom Harrison said. "See, Red, it's like this. It seldom is the things you are aware of that get you into trouble when it comes to money. To the contrary, it's the unknown, the things that you didn't even know existed that often get you. What Mister Reilly is saying is there's a lot you need to learn about certain types of people and that you need to be educated about those things."

Red thought for a moment. "I just don't know. It sounds like a good idea, but . . ."

"It is," the sheriff interrupted. "Red, that is what I wanted to discuss with you back at home." He rose from the chair and addressed the banker. "Jacob, after we look over the will and talk it over, I promise we will get it back to you and we'll let you know if we have any questions."

The banker smiled and nodded. "Sounds good, Tom. You two take care."

CHAPTER SIX

Red walked into the house, threw his hat on the table, saying: "I wish we never had found that damned gold!" He turned to look the sheriff in the eye, adding: "The Old Man might still be alive today if we hadn't."

"You can't go blaming yourself for what happened, Red," Sheriff Harrison told the boy, taking a seat at the table. "Just think how happy the Old Man would be to know that you've got money enough to take care of yourself for the rest of your life, if you're careful. I don't doubt that he always worried about what would happen to you if something happened to him. That's taken care of now, and you can pretty much do whatever you want. That don't happen very often. I can tell you that my wife Annabelle and her ma struggled something awful once her pa died. Her ma did whatever she could to make money to take care of Annabelle and her three siblings. 'Tweren't easy on any of them. Her brother died of the fever when he was just a little younger than you. Couldn't afford no doc, and they just watched him wither away day by day. Left Annabelle in a bad way for a long time she said." He stopped and just sat in silence for a few minutes before continuing.

"But in spite of that, Annabelle kept a good outlook on life. Yup, Annabelle always looked for the good side when something bad happened. What I mean is, she always said that even though you might have something terrible happen to you . . . well, you gotta keep faith and hope alive within you because you gotta go on, and, besides, you never know . . . something good could be in your future. I can't help but think that all the hardships she suffered in her young years made her stronger in the end." He paused. "Maybe she was always strong. What do I know."

Harrison got up to put on a pot of coffee. "Now in your case," he said, standing by the stove, a glowing match stick held in his fingers, "I'm assuming you have a lot of good memories of your adventures with your pa. And to top it off, except for some of the big ranchers, you're richer than most everyone in the territory." He loaded up the coffee pot. "So now, you just have to be smart with your money."

"I am smart," Red declared loudly. "I can read and write."

"Sure you are," Harrison said reassuringly. "But I doubt that you know anything about the handling of that much money."

"I thought that was Mister Reilly's job."

"It is, and he'll do an honest job of it. But someday you might want to manage your own affairs . . . buy a house, settle down, have a family, that sort of thing. I know that may seem a long way off in the future, but in the meantime if word got out about your money, every rascal in the area would come around trying to swindle you out of it. I'm afraid that after all those years out there in the hills prospecting, just the two of you . . . well, the truth is, you really don't have all that much experience in dealing with those kind of people. I'm not saying there aren't a lot of good people out there, but there are a lot of miscreants looking to take advantage of those with money."

Red pointed to his rifle and pistol which were hanging on a gun rack near the front door. "I can deal with them just fine as long as I have those."

The sheriff shook his head. "There's more to protecting yourself than just depending on a gun. But all right, let's consider that for a moment. I know your pa taught you how to shoot to feed yourself and protect yourself, but some people out there are out to take advantage of you and get at your money. A gun can't help you in that situation. . . ."

"They take my money, I'll go after them and a gun will do the talking," Red broke in angrily.

"Hold on, hold on," the sheriff advised. "If word gets out, that money could put a target on your back. I know you can survive on the frontier, but living among people is different."

"I've got no use for towns or people," Red insisted. "Me and the Old Man had a good life."

"But he's gone, Red," Harrison said kindly. "You want to live alone for the rest of your life? Wandering out there with no one to talk to or share adventures with?"

"No, but . . . ," Red said hesitantly.

"Then what are you gonna do? Just be a rich loner?"

"I . . . ," Red responded, realizing for the first time that he had to do some hard thinking about his future.

Harrison was wise enough to know he needed to keep quiet while Red let the reality of his situation sink in.

After Red considered what the lawman had said, he asked: "Maybe you could teach me? About people, I mean. I could pay you."

Tom shook his head. "I have a better idea. Back to my original proposition."

A spark of suspicion shot through Red's eyes which Sheriff Harrison saw immediately.

"Well, you stay here and live with me, I'll teach you what I've learned about people, good and bad, in my years as a lawman, but you don't pay me. You go to school and learn as much as you can. Do your best to become a part of the community of Baker's Gap. How old are you again?"

"Close to fifteen. You know, the Old Man once told me that if things seem too good to be true, they ain't true."

"And he was right," Tom agreed.

"So what's the catch?" Red asked, his curiosity getting the better of him.

Tom smiled. "You live here for at least two more years. During that time, like I said, I'll do as much as I can to help you learn about people. You'll go to school and learn about arithmetic, history, geography . . . outside the area you know like the back of your hand . . . and everything else Miss Harriet can teach you over at the school."

Red lowered his eyes, scratched his head, and then sat there, mulling it over, his arms crossed over his chest. Harrison watched him, uncertain if he had gotten his point across, afraid the boy would say no and just head out of town to be on his own again. He had to break the silence, break into the boy's thoughts.

"What weapon did you use to dispense with those two killers?"

"Used my long gun like I told you," Red replied. "It's the one I'm most comfortable with. The Old Man had a pistol, but I didn't hardly get to use it. Never had enough money to buy ammunition for it."

"Well, since you bought yourself that fancy new pistol," Harrison said, "what say we throw in lessons on that gun as part of the deal, in case you decide to become a lawman?" Harrison smiled, hoping he could lure in Red with a skill he would be interested in gaining. He was pleased with himself for coming up with the idea.

"What's this Miss . . . Harriet is it? . . . like?" Red asked.

Harrison almost let out a sigh of relief for the first time, having the feeling that Red might be swayed. "She's a nice lady, but she's as strict as a rock is hard when it comes to getting an education."

Red's expression quickly changed. "How many hours do I have to be at this school a day?"

"Not rightly sure. No matter, you'll get to like it. They got books there a-plenty."

"I guess I do have a lot to learn," Red muttered to himself, which made Tom smile. "That it?" Red asked as he pondered what, if any, his alternatives were. He quickly determined there was only one, and its appeal was diminished greatly without the company of the Old Man.

"Nope," Harrison admitted, "there's one last part to the deal. And that's you leave that pistol and rifle right where they are unless I give you permission to take them out."

Red shook his head angrily, started to get up, almost shouting: "No way am I promising that!"

"Wait a second and hear me out," Tom urged, kicking himself for bringing this last condition up before he had convinced the boy. "If you're going hunting, or we're going out to practice shooting, or any other good reason, you can carry your gun. But you can't take it to school, or carry it around town. I think that's fair."

"What if some friend of those two killers comes around and hears that I was the one . . ."

Tom put out his hand. "I'm the sheriff, remember. I don't think a young man like yourself, walking around town, would be identified as a killer of those two hardcases by someone coming into town. Hell, you'd probably be more of a target if you had a gun on you and they learned you were the one that done it. Besides, Baker's Gap is a pretty peaceful town when compared with others."

Red went back to being silent. Finally he asked: "Why are you doing this for me?"

Tom scratched his head, expelling air through pursed lips. "Don't rightly know for sure, but I know it ain't pity. . . ." He stopped. "That's not true, Red. Can I be honest with you?" Red nodded. "As I told you, I lost my son. Left a hole in my insides. Sometimes when I see a young boy . . . well, it reminds me of what I lost and I wonder what kind of man he would have grown into. Felt that when I saw you coming back into town. And now that I've gotten to know you a little better, I believe he would have been a lot like you. Don't ask me why, but I feel that. So I want to help you, because you have helped me already. I don't feel so alone when I'm with you . . . I feel like I'm with my son. I understand why the prospector took you under his wing. You've shared camp with him for most of your life. I can't replace him. But, Red, you've got the makings of a fine man in you and I want to do what I can to help in any way I can to make you that man. I think we might be good for each other."

Red put his hands on his knees awkwardly, shrugged, stood, and then stuck out his right hand. "All right. You've got a deal, Sheriff."

"Unless I'm on duty, just call me Tom from now on," he said with a big smile.

Red smiled back. "That won't be a problem at all, Tom."

For Sheriff Harrison the deal he had struck with Red was everything he had hoped it would be. The young man was helpful, and provided the companionship that had been missing from his home life for far too many years. There were many times throughout the day when the lawman would just sit back and study Red no matter what he was doing, and he would think to himself: *That's the way my Johnny would have approached that.* It didn't matter what it was, from the way Red wrinkled his brow when he was reading to the way he wiped his mouth on his sleeve when he thought no one was looking.

For Red, the transition from a nomadic life to living in a house in a town took some getting used to. But after years of living primarily on the game he and the Old Man had killed and wild onions, the dishes the women prepared for him and Tom—especially Mrs. Flagg's desserts— were a welcome experience, though he missed the spicy fare he and the Old Man had eaten near the border. Tom volunteered him to help with the maintenance of the gardens of several of the women who supplied them on a regular basis with many of the tasty dinners they feasted on. He quickly developed a taste for sugar in his coffee of which there was an endless supply that never had to be rationed.

By the end of August he felt as though he had met just about everybody in Baker's Gap, all of whom enjoyed sharing a story or two upon any chance encounter. Red suspected they were expecting to learn more about him, but he preferred to listen and then make an exit as quickly as he could. It seemed most didn't subscribe to the Western belief that one shouldn't ask questions.

The most difficult adjustment for Red was sleeping inside on a bed. He preferred sleeping in his bedroll under the stars and it took several months for him to stop sneaking out at night once Tom was asleep so he could stare into the heavens, which helped him drift off.

Tom kept his promise and, at least a couple of times a week, they would head out of town and practice shooting. He even took him to the local leather smith to be measured for a holster for his Colt Peacemaker.

"So, just how do you want to wear it?" the smith asked.

"How about making it real low like the ones I've seen in the south," Red suggested. "And maybe we could add some fancy silver conchos on it?"

The leather smith, a short, middle-aged fellow named Griff, smiled in anticipation of the price he could charge. He had already heard rumors about Red's fortune.

But Tom Harrison shook his head. "The last thing you want to do when you carry a gun is to call attention to yourself. Fancy conchos and silver studs are either the mark of a dude or a fool. There's nothing wrong with fine-tooled leather, but it should be appreciated for its workmanship and not be flashy like an advertisement."

Though disappointed, Griff nodded in agreement. "I can still make it really special, Red, if that's your wish without being . . . what's the word . . . ostentatious."

Red had no idea what that word meant so he merely shrugged. He made a mental note to ask Tom later.

"And the style and measurement?" the leather smith asked.

Yeah, what about that? Red wondered.

When Red didn't answer, Griff said: "How 'bout we make you a buscadero rig. The cartridge belt'll ride through the leather in the holster, settling the gun on your hip, level with the palm of your hand. That way when you draw, your hand will naturally cock your Colt as you raise it up."

"That the best way?" Red asked curiously.

"Hard to answer that. There are shootists who carry their gun cross-draw style while others use a twist draw with the gun butt facing forward. Others keep their pistol real low on the leg like those Texas *pistoleros* you mentioned. Some use a shoulder holster, or carry the gun square in front of their belt buckle. And if . . ."

"A buscadero rig should serve you just fine," the sheriff interjected, cutting off Griff's long-windedness.

Red looked at Tom and nodded.

"One thing's for sure," Griff said. "When I get through working on it, that there pistol of yours will come out of my greased leather holster quicker than a fox fleeing a hen house."

Tom laughed. "Not very proud of your work are you, Griff?"

"Got every right to be," he replied, sticking out his chest.

"Don't worry, Red," the sheriff agreed, patting his holster which caused a twinge in his shoulder. "He's not just blowing smoke. Griff made this here holster for me and it hasn't failed me yet. Least not in a fair fight."

So a holster was ordered. Red was excited, but a few weeks later the first day of school arrived.

Flinging his coat off onto the floor of the sheriff's office, Red announced: "I'm not going back to that school!" He yanked the chair out from in front of Tom's desk and stared unflinchingly at the lawman.

"Problem with school, Red?" Tom asked calmly.

"What's not wrong with it? I'm the oldest, the biggest, the strongest, the smartest kid in the place."

"You're the smartest, huh?" Tom said.

"Yeah, I probably am," Red snapped back. "Besides, they all stare at me. I don't like it. And the girls . . . they giggle!"

"What are you there for, Red?" Tom asked.

"Because you said I had to go to school, or have you forgotten?" he responded as he slumped down deeper into the chair and started muttering to himself.

"No, I haven't forgotten," Tom said. "But perhaps you've forgotten that we made a deal, and going to school was part of it so you could better yourself. I know you want to. You ask me all sorts of questions . . . you want to know the meaning of words, so I know you want to expand your vocabulary. You wouldn't even know that word's meaning if you hadn't asked me. Besides, in time you might make friends with some of the other students and . . ."

"Be friends with those . . . those kids? That will never happen."

His frustration growing, Tom said: "You're right. You're there to learn, not make friends. So do that," he said, getting up from the chair and grabbing his coat and hat. Before going out the door, he added: "You owe it to yourself, not to me."

Anyone else in Red's position would probably have simply quit and moved on, especially with so much money in the bank, but this boy was stubborn and had a strong sense of honor. He had shaken hands with Tom and given his word. As long as his new friend and mentor upheld his end of the bargain, Red would keep his, even if it killed him.

Resigned, Red went to school the next day, and the next, and soon he learned to just ignore the other students. As Tom had said, Miss Harriet ran her classroom of twelve students with an iron fist. He reasoned that a wagon master would probably have been more lenient than Miss Harriet. But seeing how rowdy the students could get when she left the room even for a few minutes, he understood her approach.

He found keeping up with the work on some subjects was difficult and he could have done without the homework. But several weeks in, he realized that the sheriff had been right and that he didn't know all that much. No subject captured his imagination as did history, and he was soon ordering books recommended by Miss Harriet in their after-class conversations, which grew in frequency as did his hunger to learn more. He received his first lesson in carpentry when Tom suggested they build a bookcase to house his growing collection of books. By the end of the school year his most prized volume was his dictionary and he was determined to learn the meaning and the spelling of all seventy thousand words in it. He thought this Webster fellow must be the smartest man in the world.

The conversations he had with Tom at night about what he was learning made the sheriff proud of Red's diligence. Often times Red had to teach Tom about an historical event in which he was interested so that they could talk about it, which made Tom smile. Red learned that every Saturday night when Tom would leave for a couple of hours, he was going over to the boarding house to have dinner with Miss Harriet. When he got up the nerve, he asked if they could invite Miss Harriet over to their house occasionally on those nights so he could join in the conversation. That only happened a couple of times though because Red was full of questions for Miss Harriet and he monopolized the conversation. Although Red was upset, once Tom told him that he was treating Miss Harriet like a teacher on one of her two nights off, he understood.

The bond between Red and Tom grew stronger every day, and that bond had nothing to do with the original bargain they had struck.

Baker's Gap had been relatively quiet for months. It seemed that the only men occupying the jail cells were the drunks who had gotten out of hand. For that reason Tom and Red spent a lot of time outside the city where Red practiced drawing and shooting his Peacemaker.

He'd come a long way since his first lesson once his holster had been made. Even though he was skilled with the use of a rifle, Red hadn't been that familiar with pistols.

"The idea is to make the bullets go where your eyes are looking," Tom had instructed him in the early days of the lessons, "not to make your eyes try to follow the pistol. Keep your knees slightly bent, don't lock them in place, in case you have to move quickly to the side or drop down. You have to learn how to start firing the second your hand touches the grips and the barrel clears the holster."

When Tom had quickly fired off three shots

that sounded like one to Red, he explained: "It comes from practice. Watch me. You raise your hand, keeping your thumb sideways, like this, and cock the pistol just as you pull it up out of the holster. Then as soon as the gun barrel leaves the leather, you rotate your hand up and fire right from the hip. Next, you turn your gun hand to the left, sideways, so the gun is horizontal . . . the barrel still facing forward. Then you push the gun forward, hammer tight, against your hip. You want to squeeze the trigger down, so the hammer won't lock back. It'll release and fire. Next, you turn the pistol back upright . . . like you're turning a doorknob . . . and you fan the hammer again, but this time use the side of your left hand. Do it right, the three moves are so fast they'll sound as if they were fired simultaneously."

"Can I try?" Red asked.

Tom reached over and pulled the Colt from the boy's holster. "Nope," he replied as he emptied the pistol of its bullets.

"Hey, what's the big idea?" Red said.

Tom had handed back the pistol, saying: "For the next few weeks we are going to practice drawing and dry-firing, because, first, I want you to develop reflexes that come naturally, no thinking about it all. So we're going to start by drawing slow so you don't drop the gun, and then gradually we'll begin speeding things up.

Besides, I don't want either of us to get shot in the foot by accident. I'm sort of used to having ten toes."

Red laughed. "Yeah, me too."

"Look, Red, I know you are anxious to shoot, but it's better to take it slow and steady like the tortoise and win the race, than to rush at it like the hare and lose. You have all the time in the world to learn this and I ain't going nowhere. So what do you say we just have fun with this and do it my way, no matter how long it takes."

Red shrugged. He had no idea what turtle race Tom was referring to, but he agreed on general principles.

The lessons in pistol work continued for over a year and a half and by that time Red was as gun-savvy with a revolver as he had been with a rifle. But the lessons didn't stop there. Because Red's exposure to people had been limited before coming to Baker's Gap, Harrison began teaching him all the things he had learned over the course of his career.

He taught him about set-ups, ambushes, back-shooters, hide-away or back-up guns, and the difference between shooting out on the trail versus in a town or a room, especially a crowded one like a saloon. Some of the things Tom told him had already been ingrained into him by the Old Man, while others were totally new ideas—

how to survey a room for potential problems, what could be considered suspicious behavior, and what to look for when studying people.

"Watch for a man who's always patting a pocket or adjusting a waist coat. Fellows doing that usually have a hidden weapon they're checking on," Tom told him.

The sheriff honed the boy's abilities about compensating for the sun being in your eyes and how to fire accurately when riding on horseback or even a buckboard.

Red practiced shooting with both hands, in case one was ever injured, and learned some fancy gun-handling, too, like tossing the gun from one hand to the other, or doing what was known as a road agent's spin or a border roll, a fancy move by a gun artist that made you think he was surrendering his loaded gun, grip first, but then was reversed by a flip of the gun, which put the weapon back into firing position and in the hand of the shootist.

So, while Miss Harriett drummed history, philosophy, grammar, mathematics, and geography into Red's head, Tom Harrison took every opportunity to discuss the philosophy and application of pistol craft and marshaling. It was his hope that Red would become a lawman like himself. But the sheriff always treaded lightly when discussing the subject of shooting at another man. The pair had long conversations in the evening about various scenarios that Tom had either experienced or heard about.

"It ain't enough to outdraw the other fellow," Tom would remind him often. "You have to know when to fire, and you have to hit what you aim at."

"Why? If you know you can outdraw him?"

"Well, consider this," answered Tom. "What if you come across someone standing over a dead body with a gun in his hand?"

"I draw and shoot. Right?"

"And what if that person just happened across the body, picked up the gun, and is really an innocent bystander? You draw and it'll force them to shoot back."

Red nodded. "I see what you mean. But it still helps to be quicker, doesn't it?"

"Sure it does. But the real determining factor isn't speed. It's your willingness to shoot and perhaps kill another man. You also have to be willing to take a hit and still keep on firing. It may mean the difference between life and death."

Red had become uncomfortable when Tom said that, and he mumbled to himself: "I already know that."

Tom Harrison thought a moment before saying: "Red, you went after those men in a fit of rage. I'm not saying that you did anything wrong necessarily, but in the future things may be different."

"How?" Red asked. Tom swore he could see tears welling up in the boy's eyes.

"Let me ask you a question first," Tom replied. "Of all the weapons you have at your disposal, do you know what the most important one is?"

Red thought about the question. "Still my rifle probably."

"Nope. Try again."

Red couldn't figure it out. "What is it?"

"Your brain," Tom answered.

"My brain?" Red repeated.

"Look here, in a fight it's the man who keeps his focus and stays in control and doesn't lose his temper who walks away," Tom explained. "You were damned lucky going up against those murderers, and I'm not referring to the fact that you were so young. That said, even though you were filled with hate at the time, you still won against those men because you had thought out a plan. But you also had a whole heap of luck."

"Weren't all luck," Red contradicted Tom.

"You aren't listening to me, Red," Tom replied. "I believe I said, first, that you had a plan. But, I guess I did leave out the fact that you had a whole heap of guts."

CHAPTER SEVEN

It was the end of Red's second year of school. It was with regret that he said good bye to Miss Harriet as his teacher, though if he stayed in Baker's Gap he knew he would still visit with her to discuss his favorite subject, history, and maybe even join in on her Saturday night dinners with Tom, if he didn't bombard her with questions.

As he made his way home slowly, Red thought about the bargain he had struck with Tom a little over two years ago. They had both kept up their half of the bargain, and the rewards had been larger than either had expected. But now that he was almost seventeen, he felt a growing desire to do something with his life.

That night, over dinner, Tom set his fork and knife down, and looked at Red, saying: "Have you given any thought to what you want to do now that your school days are over? I know money isn't a concern, but I can't imagine you plan on just sitting around Baker's Gap doing nothing for the rest of your years."

It was at that moment that everything clarified in his thoughts, and Red realized that he had made up his mind about his future almost as soon as he had ridden out that day after the men who had murdered the Old Man. Riding back after the showdown, he had vowed to himself that someday he was going to try to stop as many outlaws as he could and right wrongs. And after he had met Tom and learned that he was a lawman who was highly respected for his abilities, Red had instinctively known that he could learn things from the sheriff that might be of use in the future.

"I have thought too much about it, Tom. Truth is I've known all along what I intend to do with the rest of my life."

"Care to let me in on the secret?" Tom asked.

"I'm going to be a lawman," Red declared.

Tom frowned. "I know I mentioned that as a possibility a long way back, but I hope you've really thought about it hard. It's not an easy life and it's often one that's far too short."

"I'm aware of that," Red replied.

Sheriff Harrison thought a moment and chuckled. "I was also going to say it's not a very good way to get rich, but I guess you've got that part already covered, haven't you?"

Red smiled back. "Yeah, I guess I have. Lucky, huh?"

The lawman nodded. "I'd say so. Well, if you're really sure about this, I guess it's time to start taking you along on my rounds. Next level of training, so to speak."

Red smiled. "Sounds good to me. And I get to carry a gun now, right?" Red asked.

"I guess so, but only when you're with me," Tom said sternly.

"That's good, because if I'm on rounds with you, and something like a gunfight starts up, and you get hit . . . ," Red said.

"Why are you so fired up to get me shot?" Tom interrupted.

"I'm not," Red said.

"Then what is it? Why are you so anxious to step in harm's way?"

Red hesitated a moment before answering. "I guess it's just that I don't want to be a helpless victim like Pa was when we came to town. I don't want to go face down in the street without even having a chance. I want to prevent that from happening to others, too."

"I got shot that day, too, if you'll remember. Carrying a gun doesn't guarantee you anything," the sheriff pointed out. "Besides, your pa was armed, right?"

"But he wasn't expecting trouble, so he wasn't prepared. His gun was with the horses," Red reminded Tom.

"Look, Red," Tom said, reaching out and putting his hand on the lad's shoulder. "A gun is a tool, no more, no less. It's as good or as bad as the man handling it. Remember, firearms have different purposes . . . long-range rifles are for hunting, pistols for self-defense, guns for sport target competition, and shotguns for crowd control or to protect a stagecoach. But they're just tools. Now, you don't see a young carpenter getting all fired up about carrying around his saw or his hammer, do you?"

"I've seen you admire many a new gun," Red stated.

"Yes, I have, just as I'm pretty sure a master carpenter would admire a brand new finely made and well-balanced hammer."

"Yeah, I suppose, but nothing is as good for protection as a gun. I don't think I'm ever likely to see a bank robbery being carried out or stopped with a hammer."

"Nope," Tom agreed, smiling. "But remember, the Comanches, Apaches, and Kiowas do pretty well in battle, even without any guns."

"Some have breech-loaders. So why are you saying this now . . . after all you've taught me? Why do you even bother to carry when you make your rounds as sheriff?" Red asked.

"I didn't necessarily say go unarmed all the time," Tom replied. "I said keep your head screwed on straight about it. I carry because a firearm is the right tool for the job I have. I just want you to be safe, and that means making sure you don't get all fired up about shooting someone."

Red seemed truly offended. "That what you think I'm doing?"

The sheriff looked at him, wondering himself

why he was trying to dissuade the boy from a job he had been preparing him for. "No, I know you're not. I just wanted it said out loud is all."

Red nodded. "Don't worry, Tom. I get it. Besides, not much has happened in Baker's Gap since you and Pa got shot."

"That's true enough. But you never know. So, if you're ready, we might as well get started," Tom announced as he pushed back his chair and stood up.

That night the two walked the town together. Being Thursday, it was especially quiet.

As they approached a corner, they heard a muffled sound.

"Remember, Red, my job is to keep the peace, not start a war. Sometimes what you see or even hear might have to be ignored for the greater good. It often boils down to a making a judgment call, and that's where experience comes in. That's why sometimes what you say can be as important as what you do."

Once they turned the corner, they saw Charlie Kohl, drunk as usual, leaning over a dog, his face buried in the dog's neck and making undecipherable sounds.

"Nothing unusual here," Tom commented as they walked around Charlie and the dog.

"What'd you mean about talking can be more important than doing something when you're trying to arrest somebody?" the teenager asked.

"Well, let's say you want to pat someone down to check for a hidden weapon, or maybe you want to handcuff a suspect. Sometimes you just need to tell the fellow to turn around slowly and keep his hands in sight. A lawman is more likely to be successful if he speaks calmly but cautiously, rather than by snapping orders and trying to push the fellow around."

"Why do you think that is?" Red asked. "I mean, you're the law . . . doesn't that raise the hackles on the back of anyone you approach?"

Tom smiled. "I suppose it does if he's guilty of something. But think about how you would react if I started pushing you around and barking orders at you, especially if you were alone on a dark street. Or if I did the same to a drunken cowboy."

"I guess I'd start swinging my fists," Red said.

"Exactly. It's more than likely that will get you in a fight, or worse. You might be trying to stop a potential problem, but how you approach the problem can change the outcome. It's often not what you say, but how you say it."

They continued on their way through the streets of Baker's Gap. They walked alleyways and checked doors to make sure they were locked and showed no sign of having been jimmied. From time to time they would stop in at the saloon to be sure no one was too deep in their cups and becoming belligerent.

"I like a drink as well as the next man, I suppose," Tom said, "but as I've said before, my job is to keep the peace here. Some men just have a drink or two to relax. They're harmless. Unfortunately, others tend to overdo it and some of them can't handle it."

"And that's when we step in?" Red asked.

The sheriff shook his head. "Not necessarily. Some get what I call happy drunk. They become friends with everyone in the bar, have a good time, maybe get a little too frisky around the saloon girls. The ladies who work there expect a little nonsense from the customers, but they usually know how to handle it. But some men get mean drunk. Don't know exactly why it is, but after they start drinking, they go looking to pick a fight, feel everyone is against them. They become argumentative and are quick to anger."

"Are those the ones we arrest?" Red asked eagerly.

"Those are the ones we keep an eye on," the sheriff informed him. "A mean drunk can be dangerous and unpredictable. You can't rationalize with them as easily as a sober man. Who knows what goes through a particular drunk's mind. One minute they're arguing and the next minute they're either going for a weapon or throwing up on your boots."

"Go through a lot of boots, do you?" Red asked, and laughed.

"Not yet," Tom answered as they entered the Broken Arrow. Stopping at the entry, Tom looked around, then asked Red: "Do you notice anything that bothers you?"

Red's eyes traveled carefully from one side of the room to the other, pausing to look at each man. As far as he was concerned, nothing looked out of the ordinary. There were men playing cards at several round tables. Toward the back was a small riser where a slightly older but still attractive blonde woman was singing. Nearby, several customers had turned their chairs around to face her, singing or mouthing along with her as she sang.

"Everything looks all right to me," Red said.

"Maybe," Tom muttered. "What about that fellow over to your right? I don't recognize him."

"That one?" Red replied. He was getting ready to point, but the sheriff pushed his arm down.

"Yeah that one. But don't point."

"You know him? Is he wanted?

Tom shook his head. "Not so far as I know. But look around. Compare the look on his face compared to everyone else. That man is sitting alone with an almost empty whiskey bottle on his table and a full glass in his hand."

"Do we arrest him?" Red asked.

"No reason to. But without being obvious, look

at his face. Doesn't look very happy now, does he?"

"No, I guess not."

"That's what I mean when I tell you, you have to get a feel for people."

"So what do we do? Do we go over there? Maybe ask him what's doin'?"

Tom shook his head. "Do that and you're asking for trouble, unless you want him to know he's being watched. He hasn't broken the law here . . . yet. Remember we're here to stop problems, not start them. A sheriff who shows up and braces an innocent man, drunk or not, is just looking for a fight. We'll just watch for a while. Pretend we're taking in the show. But we'll keep an eye on him."

It appeared to be a false alarm when, a half hour later, the drunk reached over to take his coat off the chair and stood. At the same time a waiter with a tray of beers walked past the loner's table and stumbled, spilling beer on the man.

"Why you stupid oaf. Them's my best boots!" the man yelled.

Backing up, the waiter was overly apologetic. "It was an accident, sir. I tripped. I am truly sorry."

Slowly, Tom started moving toward the fellow, Red following close behind. "Red, keep that hogleg of yours holstered unless I tell you otherwise," he said over his shoulder.

"Sorry!" the drunk said to the waiter. "That doesn't fix the problem, but this will." Taking a step back, he was clearly reaching for his pistol when Tom drew his.

"Don't even think about it, mister," Tom hissed.

Red was expecting a shoot-out, but Tom moved forward as the drunk was distracted, and spun the pistol in his hand, slamming it, butt down, on the loner's head. The drunk's gun fell from his hand as he collapsed.

"Take his gun, Red," was the sheriff's next order.

Red did as instructed.

"It was an accident, Sheriff. It wasn't my fault," the waiter explained nervously.

"I know it was. It's not your fault. I know the difference between an accident and an 'on purpose.'" Tom smiled, pulling a pair of hand-cuffs from his back pocket. He handed them to Red.

"Put them on him before he wakes up. Make sure they're locked."

Red squatted and did as he was told. "They're good, Tom. Do you think he'll die?"

"No," Tom answered, then turned to the waiter. "Sam, could you get me a pitcher of water and a mop."

"Sure, Sheriff. Coming right up."

Red was a little confused as to why Tom would want a pitcher of water. He for one wasn't thirsty.

And why would he need a mop? His question was answered once Sam returned.

Tom took the pitcher and turned it upside down right over the drunk, emptying its contents on the unconscious man's head. That explained the need for a mop.

As the man came to, spitting and wiping his face, Tom hoisted him off the floor. Assisted by Red, Tom hauled the drunk to the jail where they deposited him in a cell. When asked, he told Tom his name.

"Was a good night," Tom said as he dropped into the chair behind his desk. "Everyone went home alive, including this here, fellow"—he cocked his head in the direction of the cells—"and what little damage he received isn't permanent."

Red was clearly impressed with Tom's calm in what could have been a bad situation. "What now?" he asked.

"Well, you should head home," the lawman said, settling his legs on top of the desk. "I'll be there in a couple of hours. Since Miss Harriet says you read and write so well now, I want you to go through my collection of Wanted posters early tomorrow morning to see if there are any warrants out on this jasper before we let him go. That way when we talk to him, we'll know if he's lying or not. I hope he's a good man and just a bad drunk. Sometimes, however, they turn out to be both bad men and bad drunks. Maybe you'll find out ahead of time by going through the posters."

Red groaned at the thought of all that paperwork, but having seen Tom at his desk at all hours, he knew that was part of the job of being a lawman.

"Don't fuss on it," Tom said. "Besides, going through all those posters and memorizing them might help you recognize an outlaw someday when you see one."

CHAPTER EIGHT

It was the heart of a hot summer and Baker's Gap was seeing more than its share of strangers passing through. Tom was pleased that the towns-folk had accepted Red's new role as unofficial deputy, especially since many had felt originally that Red might be too hot-headed for the job. But after he responded to a few minor incidents, Red had proven he could be level-headed, and it didn't take long for the most critical to commend Tom for taking on the young man.

One afternoon Tom told Red to head over to the Broken Arrow saloon.

"As I was passing by the doors, the barkeep glanced at me. Now maybe it was nothing, maybe just my imagination, but could be something is up," the sheriff told Red.

"So let's get going," Red replied eagerly.

"I have to attend to another problem, so I've got to send you over alone. You all right with that?"

"What problem?" Red asked.

"Luke Townsend said he's been losing a couple of head off his place now and then. Might be they just wandered off into the bush, but it could be rustlers . . . white or red. A few other ranchers have mentioned losses from their herds, too, so

I figure I better go check it out. I trust you'll be able to handle things here. Just remember what I taught you," Tom cautioned.

"I know, don't be overconfident," Red said as he took his rig off the wall peg in the sheriff's office. "You be careful too, Tom," he said as he buckled on his holster. "Just because we haven't had any Indian trouble in a while doesn't mean all's quiet out there."

"I will," Tom replied, pulling his Winchester out from the gun rack. "See you later, Red." After checking the rifle one last time, the sheriff walked out the door and was riding out of town ten minutes later.

Red took a deep breath and then walked down the street to the Broken Arrow. As he neared the door, he heard glass smashing and yelling coming from inside. When a gun shot went off, Red released the holster thong from his sidearm's hammer before pushing through the bat-wing doors.

Facing him were two tough-looking men at the bar, waving their six-guns in the air. At a table off to the left was a nondescript and slightly older man with a long shaggy beard and a beat up old Texican-style sombrero. Red quickly made him out to be an out-of-work old cowpoke. He was obviously of little consequence. The others in the bar were locals.

"All right, boys. You've had your fun, now put

the guns away." He directed this to the two by the bar.

" 'Boys' he says," said the shorter of the two. "Since when does a snot-nosed kid like you tell real men what to do?" Both of the men wore their holsters low down on the leg, Texas style. It was clear they'd had one too many drinks.

"When he's the deputy sheriff in town, he does," Red said, shifting his vest to reveal his badge. "Now just put your guns down and let's call it a day."

The taller of the pair shook his head. Red failed to notice the glimmer in the man's eyes as he stared back at him. "No, sonny, I don't think so. I think maybe you ought to drop yours."

Red felt confident he could take on the two men if he had to, but first he'd try to get them to put away their guns. What he hadn't anticipated was the gun barrel that was suddenly poking him in his back.

"Drop the hogleg, sonny," the man said, leaning in close to Red's ear.

Red could smell the sweat emanating from the man as he leaned in. Turning ever so slightly, Red caught a glance at the large man behind him. Red didn't feel that he had a choice, so he slowly pulled his gun and placed it gently on the nearest table.

The man came around from behind and joined his two partners at the bar. "We haven't plugged a lawman in what . . . five months is it, Sid?" The other two men smiled as they leaned back against the bar.

" 'Bout that. What say we shoot him on the count of three," the third man suggested.

His confidence decreasing each second, Red considered his options as quickly as he could, but try as he might, he could find no way out of this predicament.

"Sounds good to me," the tallest man called Sid said with a grin. "We all shoot on three." The other two pursed their lips and nodded. "One," Sid said with a sneer on his face.

"Two," the shortest man said calmly.

Red swallowed as he realized he was going to die just as the old-timer he'd seen when he entered the saloon stood up out of his chair and faced toward the door.

"Whoa, there," he said, looking at the three men and raising up his hands. "Hold on jush a minute, hoss." He was clearly drunk, his words slurring together. "Wait jush a gosh-darned minute till I gets out of thish here place," he said, hiccupping as he turned back toward the door nearly losing his balance. "Y'all can per-perforates him all you want oncet I's gone, but I don't want no holes in my old carcass." He wobbled as he wound his way around the tables, knocking glasses off tables and bumping into chairs which he attempted to use for support.

The three toughs laughed at his antics, for-getting about Red as they watched.

"Sure thing, old-timer. We'll wait for you," Sid managed to get out, laughing and slapping his leg.

The old man stumbled a few more times, then, as he passed Red, he stumbled again, this time shoving the deputy off to the side with his left hand as hard as he could.

"Three," the old-timer said as he drew his gun and spun back around. Before Red even knew what was happening the old drunk was firing his pistol, fanning from right to left. The shots rang out practically as one and the three men fell to the floor in front of the bar like a row of dominoes. There was no doubt in Red's mind that all three were dead. The bullets had all hit dead center.

The old man replaced the gun in his holster, walked over to Red and, now as sober as a judge, offered him a hand up. Red couldn't believe how convincingly the fellow had faked being drunk.

"Thank you, mister. I'm eternally grateful," Red said as he brushed off his clothes.

"You're welcome," the stranger said, spitting his chaw into a nearby spittoon.

"Just who are you?" Red asked in wonderment. He was more amazed by what he had witnessed than he was relieved at still being upright and alive.

"Al Thornton," the man replied. "Texas Ranger

Al Thornton. My real name's Aloysius Burnside Thornton, but no one ever called me that except my ma, and that was only when I was in trouble for one thing or another." He smiled. "You ever call me that I might have to take you out to the wood shed."

"T-Texas Ranger?" Red stammered. "What are you doing in Baker's Gap?"

"You mean besides saving your life?" he asked, and grinned.

The deputy turned an even darker shade of red than the river after which he had been named. "Yeah, besides that," he replied with embarrassment.

"Two reasons. First I was trailing those three, wanted for a string of robberies and a couple of assaults."

"And the other?" Red asked.

"Thought I might look up an old friend of mine," he replied.

Red turned to the barkeep. "John, can you send someone over to the undertaker to make arrangements for these fellows? Tell him I'll come around later."

"Sure thing, Red . . . er, um . . . Deputy," the man said, still shaking a little from what had just transpired in his saloon.

"I've got some coffee in the office if you'd care to join me," Red said politely.

"Sounds good. Don't forget your pistol,

Deputy," Ranger Thornton said, and turned so the young man wouldn't see his smile of amusement.

Red felt heat rising to his face as he realized he had almost walked out without his gun. He heard snickering from a few of the customers. Humiliated, he swiped it up from the table and then followed the Ranger out the door. When he caught up to his side, pointing, he said: "The sheriff's office is over this way."

Al Thornton nodded. "I know. Been here before."

A few minutes later, Red was putting the coffee pot on the stove as Thornton took a seat in one of the chairs in front of the desk.

"Why'd you have to tackle those men alone? You seem a bit young. Where's the sheriff?" the Ranger asked.

Red bristled at the reference to his age, but answered calmly: "Sheriff's out of town looking into some possible rustling. We figured I could handle anything that came up."

"Mind taking a little advice then?"

Red shook his head. "From a Ranger, I'd appreciate it."

"Good . . . shows you have sense. Some folks don't like hearing any kind of criticism."

"Mister, you just saved my life. Don't think I'm in a position to get all het up."

"First of all, if you ever hear gunshots in a place you intend entering, use the back door. Gives you a time to assess the lay of the land before being seen."

"What if there's no back door?"

"Well, then"—Thornton stroked his beard—"try peeking through a front window first, then when you go in, slide to the right or left of the door, keeping close to it while you survey things. Finally, iffen you have to go it alone, a shotgun is a lot more useful as well as intimidating than a six-shooter."

"But a scatter-gun only has two shots and today there were three men."

"True, but one look at a sawed-off gun, most men will think twice about starting anything. It's a powerful dissuader."

"And if I don't have a scatter-gun with me . . . like today?"

"Whether you carry one or not, a lawman is always smart to wear a small hidden back-up on his person . . . pocket revolver, derringer. Keep it in your boot or tucked in somewhere so it's out of view. Might make the difference between living and dying if your primary weapon fails or is taken away." He cocked an eyebrow at Red.

"That makes sense," Red replied, ignoring the look from the Ranger. "Was there anything else you saw that I should have done differently?"

Thornton nodded. "Don't be such a damned hero. Try not to go in alone without anyone to back you up once you hear shooting. You'll live longer."

Red was mulling over all that the Ranger had said, when, without thinking, he blurted out: "Hey, wait a minute. You said before you were trailing these three outlaws, right?"

"Yep. So?"

"Well, you went in after them alone, didn't you?" Red asked.

"There's a difference."

"What? Your age?" Red was aggravated by the thought that the Ranger felt he was too young for this kind of work.

"Not what I was thinking. At your age I was punching cows for MacAllister."

"Then what's the difference?"

Al Thornton simply replied: "I'm a Texas Ranger."

CHAPTER NINE

The two were sitting in the office, drinking coffee. Thornton was getting ready to head out, when Red said: "If you don't mind staying in town a while, I'd like you to meet my friend the sheriff . . . Sheriff Tom Harrison. He's been teaching me the trade. That's how I got to be his unofficial deputy."

"That so?" Thornton said, attempting to hold back a smile.

"And you know, he's probably the only man I ever met who might be able to match you on the draw. But, first, I have to fill out a report about what happened today." Red reached in a drawer and pulled out a sheet of paper which he shoved across the desk to Thornton. "Could you write down the names of those three men for me . . . for the report. When the sheriff gets back, I'll have him look it over and he can let you know if he has any questions." Red waited while Thornton wrote. "Are you staying in town for the night, Mister Thornton?"

"I suspect he will have questions," Al commented. "And yes, I planned on staying the night. Already checked into the hotel."

Red got an idea. "Why don't you come over to the house for dinner tonight? I'll have Sheriff

Harrison read over the report once he gets in, and if he has any questions, he can ask you tonight?"

"I guess I can do that," Al said. "What time?"

Red grinned widely, excited about introducing Tom to this Ranger. "The sheriff should be back around five, I'm guessing, so why don't we say seven at the house?"

"See you then," Thornton said as he put on his hat and stood up.

"Anybody can tell you how to get to the house," Red said as Thornton headed out the door.

Tom Harrison got back to the office right before five. Hanging up his hat, he informed Red: "Couldn't find any sure sign of rustlers. Don't rightly know what's going on with his herd, but for the time being we're just gonna take a wait-and-see approach. How'd your day go?"

Red saw that Tom looked tired and he was hesitant to tell him about the incident at the saloon, so he just handed him the report he had written up. He made himself busy, sweeping up the office as Tom read it carefully. To Red's surprise, when Tom was finished reading, he set the report on his desk and said: "You were lucky that Texas Ranger was there, Red."

"I know I was. That's why I thought you might want to meet him"—Red paused—"so I asked him to dinner tonight." Red waited for Tom to explode, but he didn't.

"Let's go home and see what we can rustle up for dinner," Tom said, clapping his hands together and heading out the door with more of a bounce in his step than Red had seen for some time.

Ranger Al Thornton arrived as the clock chimed seven. As Red ushered him inside, Tom emerged from his bedroom at the back of the house. He had a new shirt on and his gray hair was freshly combed. He smiled from ear to ear as he hurried enthusiastically across the room, saying: "Al Thornton, you old horse thief! Am I glad to see you."

"Howdy, rookie. Nice to see you still in one piece," Al said as the two pumped hands.

"You know each other?" Red asked, looking from one to the other.

"Sure do," Tom said.

"I told you I had two reasons for coming to this here town," Al reminded Red. "Those outlaws was one, but seeing my old protégé, Sheriff Tom Harrison, was the other. Speaking of old, what's with all that gray hair on your noggin, Tom? You're nearly half my age."

"I wish I was that young. As for the gray hair, it's a family curse," Tom responded as he ran a hand through his hair. "My pa was gray by the time he was thirty."

"Excuse me," Red said, his impatience growing

as he tried to figure out what was going on. "Why didn't either one of you tell me you knew each other? And what did you mean by protégé, Mister Thornton?"

"Hell's bells, boy, back in the day I done taught Tom everything I knew about being a lawman. Well, almost everything," Ranger Thornton said, laughing.

"Al, come into the parlor here and let me pour you a little Who-Hit-John," Tom suggested. "Red, you get the table ready while Al tells me all about what he's doing here in Baker's Gap. Also, I've got a few questions about want happened here this morning at the saloon."

Red felt irritated at being left out, but he scurried to get the food on so he could be part of the conversation.

Over dinner, the sheriff explained how Red had come to live with him. "You see, Al, Red here is my unofficial deputy. I've been passing along to him a lot of the things you taught me years back."

"Guess you missed a few of them, Tom," Thornton said, winking at Red, which embarrassed the young man all over again.

As Al was finishing up his second bowl of stew and several biscuits slathered in butter, Al glanced at Red as he addressed his old friend. "Tom, the lad here made a few tenderfoot mistakes today, but I have to hand it to him. Even outgunned and disarmed, he didn't back down. I never saw him flinch even once. He stared those three killers right in the eye and was prepared to take whatever was coming like a man."

"Get to know him better, Al, and you'll find he can be as stubborn and tough as a Missouri mule," Tom joked even though he was dead serious. "I do believe he has potential. I never saw a boy his age so firm in his convictions. There ain't a bit of back up in him as far as I can tell, especially if he thinks he's in the right."

"I ain't no boy," Red pointed out angrily, not sure how to handle the criticism or the flattery coming from the two older men.

"Well, from what you've told me, Al, I guess Red learned a lesson today. Maybe if he keeps it up, he might actually make it one day."

"Make what?" Red asked.

"Make it to being a grandpa," the two lawmen said almost at the same time.

Although Red laughed along with Tom and Al over the comment, he failed to see the humor in it.

Once dinner was over, he cleared the table and did the dishes, while the two old friends went out on the porch to enjoy a couple of cigars and more than a few drinks before calling it a night.

The next morning the three met up at Edith's Eatery, since Al had planned on leaving before

113

noon. The conversation had been light-hearted as the two older men regaled Red with stories of their adventures together, including Tom's stint as a Ranger.

"I didn't know you were a Ranger, Tom," Red said.

"Wasn't for long. It was after Annabelle and Johnny . . . well, you know. I met Al here, and he took me under his wing, taught me most of what I know about being a lawman. So when he joined up with the Rangers, I did, too. Spending that much time in the saddle and being constantly on the move didn't suit me. Eventually made my way here, so I could put down some roots." As Al nodded, Tom paused and then clapped his hands together. "Al, you showing up has got me to thinking."

"Well, that'd be a first," Al teased.

Red smiled to himself at the deep affection these two friends had for each other. It reminded him of the back-and-forth verbal banter between the Old Man and himself that made up a good part of their daily conversations.

"Seriously, Al," Tom continued. "It seems Red here is determined to be a lawman. And like I said, once he sets his mind on something, he can be particularly stubborn about it. Why, when he first showed up here with his pa . . ." Tom stopped and looked at Red to gauge his reaction, knowing how the subject bothered him.

When Red nodded, Tom continued: "Anyway, some cheating over at the saloon escalated into a shoot-out and Red's pa got shot and killed by a bullet that was intended for me. I got hit, too, and couldn't go after the shooters. Red, here, took it into his own hands and went after those two. And he got both of them. Wasn't quite fifteen at the time."

Al looked at Red, who was taking a bite of the doughnut Edith had made this morning, with new eyes.

"I figure Red's going to have to find some place to ply his trade," Tom was saying. "I know he doesn't have a lot of experience under his belt. But out on the trail, you'd be hard pressed to find someone with a keener eye. You showing up here, Al, seems fortuitous to me."

"Wait. What? Why can't I stay here?" Red said, in spite of the fact that he had been thinking for some time that he would have to leave Baker's Gap to fulfill his desire to be a lawman.

"Don't misunderstand, Red," Tom said. "I'd hate to see you leave, but I'm not nearly as long in the tooth as Al here is, so I'm not planning on retiring any time soon. You know this town can't even afford to pay you anything for your deputy work."

"Have I been complaining? I don't need to be paid!" Red stated a little too loudly.

"You know Baker's Gap isn't going to satisfy

someone like you with big dreams for long," Tom told him.

"What do you mean . . . someone like me?" Red asked, his heart starting to beat a little faster.

"You have skills, son," Tom said, "that are being wasted here. You want to right wrongs. Do you think you can fulfill your dreams in Baker's Gap? Will you be satisfied being my deputy?"

Red thought about it for a moment. "No, I guess not."

"So what you got in mind, Tom?" Al asked.

"Well, I'm thinking Red's suited for the life of Ranger. And if you're willing to put in a good word for him and take him on . . . the way you did with me, this might be the perfect opportunity for him to get on with the next stage of his dream of being a lawman."

Thornton studied Tom for a moment as he thought. "Well, I've taken care of Taggert and his two cohorts, so I am headed back to camp. Now I can't make any promises, especially due to your age, Red, but there might be some rookie work you could do around the camp as you learn more about being a Ranger."

"I'm no rookie," Red protested, shooting a dark look at the Ranger.

Thornton squinted as if he were looking at him for the first time. "No, I guess you're Jim Bridger, Kit Carson, Daniel Boone, and Davy Crockett all rolled up into one."

"For what it's worth, Al," Tom said, "I can tell you that for someone his age when I first met him, he knew more about the trailing men than any grown man I ever met. He lived out on the land with that old prospector from the time he was a baby, literally, until he ended up in Baker's Gap. Knows the land like the back of his hand. He tracked and took care of those two killers who murdered his pa. I'm a witness to his skills and his ability and willingness to learn. And despite what happened today, I'd trust him with my life."

"I'll be the south end of a north-bound mule," Al said. "I never heard you praise anyone like that before, Tom. Could be that it would work out."

Red didn't say anything as the two men discussed him as if he wasn't even there.

Al sat back thinking the proposition over, as Red held his breath, waiting to see what the Ranger would say next.

"I'm working with the Texas Battalion, Red," he finally said, leaning in closer to the boy. "I'm thinking that, if what Tom says is true . . . and I can't say I've ever doubted his word . . . there might be a place for you with the Rangers. So, like I already said, I can't make any promises that they'll take you on, but I'm headed back to camp and I'm willing to take you back with me. It will be up to the captain."

"It's settled then," Tom declared, leaning back in his chair.

"Do I get any say in the matter? Ask any questions?" Red asked, not quite sure what to think about the matter.

"Nope," the two men said as one.

CHAPTER TEN

Red found it difficult to concentrate as he kept thinking about the decision that had been made about his future. He hated to leave Tom, but, well, duty called. Thornton had agreed to take Red to meet the captain and had wanted to leave right away since he had dispensed with the three toughs. But Red asked for an extra day, saying that before leaving town he'd need time to say his good byes and work out some matters. When asked what those were, however, he refused to elaborate.

That afternoon Red went over to the bank when Tom was busy. He wanted to talk to the manager without the sheriff knowing about it.

"Hello, Red. It's nice to see you," Jacob Reilly said as Red took a seat.

"Nice to see you too, Mister Reilly. Some things have happened pretty fast. I'm going to be leaving Baker's Gap and I wanted to say good bye and make a few arrangements."

Reilly looked surprised. He sat up straight, saying: "You're leaving us, Red?" The possibility of losing the business of such an important customer concerned the manager. Besides, he had come to be fond of Red over the last two years.

"Yeah, I am. I'm trying to join the Rangers. Planning to head out tomorrow," Red replied.

"I heard about that trouble down at the saloon. That have anything to do with your decision?" Mr. Reilly asked.

"Indirectly," Red explained. "But not in the way you might think. The man who helped me out of that tight is a good friend of Tom's, and he's a Ranger. Tom reckons he'll be able to teach me a lot more about being a professional lawman. I know I'll miss the people here in Baker's Gap, but Tom's right . . . there really isn't much future for me here."

The manager nodded. "So what can we do for you? I hope you're not planning to close out your accounts."

"No. I trust you'll continue to take good care of it, Mister Reilly. I've got no problems with the bank. Some folks say you should never trust a bank, but I've got no complaints. You've invested my money wisely and I'm happy to leave it here."

Reilly smiled, obviously relieved. "So what is it you need then?"

Red leaned in as if sharing a secret. "This is just between you and me, right?" Jacob Reilly nodded. "I want Tom to be taken care of. He's been real good to me and I can never repay his kindness, his friendship, and all that he's taught me."

"Tom is indeed a fine man," Reilly agreed. "And a damned good lawman. So what do you have in mind?"

"Can you arrange to pay off his house, and then put two thousand dollars in an account for him?"

"I can do that. But don't you want to let him know it's paid off?"

Red shook his head. "He'd never accept it. You know that. He'd consider it charity."

"So we keep it a secret from him?" Reilly asked.

"Yes, just let him keep paying for his house and put the payments in the account with the two thousand. That way, if anything happens, he'll be taken care of. If he comes onto hard times, just have the city council say it was a bonus for his years of service . . . or some other excuse. If he stays on the job, well, it'll be there for him down the road and I'm sure he'll figure it out, but it'll be too late for him to do anything about it."

Reilly bobbed his head. "We can do that, but you know he'll never believe it's a bonus from the city . . . even you know they're always short on funds. Nonetheless, rest assured, I'll see to it, Red. You're growing into quite a man." Reilly paused. "No, let me rephrase that. You're already a good one."

"I'd also like you to start up an account for Miss Harriett, the schoolteacher . . . say three hundred. She was a good teacher and she became my friend. Don't know what her prospects are . . . I suppose she could get a husband, but I believe she's married to her profession and she'll stay on here. I figure this might make her more comfortable in her later years."

Reilly smiled. "I'd agree with you, she's an asset to the community. So anything else?"

"Just make sure no one ever finds out about these accounts until they're needed. Oh, I'd like to have some cash with me, since I don't know whether the Rangers will take me on or not."

"Of course," Reilly said as he waved over one of the tellers.

That taken care of, the two shook hands and said good bye.

Early the next morning, Red and Al prepared to leave. For Red, saying good bye to Tom was the hardest. They stood outside the sheriff's office, hemming and hawing, until Texas Ranger Al Thornton advised the two it was time to go. They shook hands, wished each other luck and good health. Red was just about to mount up, but then he turned and went back to Tom and gave him a big hug.

As Tom walked into the office, he stopped to blow his nose and take one last look as Red and Al rode out of Baker's Gap. He knew it would be a long time before either of them would return.

Thornton still had reservations about Red's skills, in spite of what Tom had told him about the young man. But because the Ranger didn't want to base his opinion on what he had seen in the saloon, he kept a close eye on Red, observing closely, evaluating his skills in an effort to determine how he handled himself on the open trail. He soon came to the conclusion that Tom hadn't been exaggerating.

He learned a lot about Red over the course of the journey in their talks at night, and he believed by the end that he had fairly good appreciation of Red's attributes as well as an awareness of his weaknesses.

It took twelve long days of pushing hard and spending long hours in the saddle to reach B camp of the Texas Battalion, Thornton's camp.

As the camp came into view, it was a beehive of activity. Thornton pointed to a wagon at the edge of camp. "Looks like you'll be meeting with Major Jones, the commander of the entire battalion, instead of Captain Barnes. I'll tell you he's not your typical leader. He's out in the field, moving from camp to camp, checking on conditions all the time. Visits the camps and travels the border with that there wagon escorted by as many as thirty men."

"Will I meet him right away?" Red asked.

"No. I'll let you get something to eat while I go and talk to him. You be all right with that?"

"I guess so," Red replied.

Once the horses were put in the corral,

Thornton showed Red to the mess tent. When Red was done eating, he went outside to sit, getting nervous as he waited. He noticed a couple of the younger men eyeing his gun and holster. Finally, Thornton appeared outside a tent some distance away and waved him over.

Red wiped his sweaty hands on his pants before stepping inside the tent.

"This here is Major John B. Jones, Red," Thornton announced.

"Pleased to meet you, sir," Red said, extending his hand.

The major remained in his chair as he shook Red's hand. "Sit, both of you," he instructed. "So Thornton here tells me you're interested in Ranger work. He also tells me you're a born tracker and an excellent horseman. We've got six camps in our battalion that cover nearly four hundred miles of frontier border from the Red River to the Nueces. With all the Indian activity these days, we keep pretty busy. And when we aren't doing that, we get a chance to do some relaxing, like going after bank robbers and murderers." He smiled and winked at Thornton.

"Sounds good to me, Major," Red said, observing that while the major was not a large man, his manner demanded respect.

"You think Thornton gave me an accurate description of you or do you think he's a mite addlepated."

"Addlepated, sir?" Red questioned, trying to recall the definition from his dictionary.

"You know"—he tapped the side of his head—"touched in the head." The major eased back in the chair and laughed before continuing. "Anyway, if you're as land savvy as Thornton here says, I'm thinking you might be useful as a courier. You'd take messages between the camps . . . let us know about the conditions out there . . . look for signs of Indians or any other potential problems. How does that sound?"

"Good, sir, real good."

"Well then, I guess if Al is willing to work with you, we can take you on for a couple of months. See how you do. With all that's been happening lately we can always use another man." The major looked Red up and down. "Or maybe make that three-fourths of a man."

When Thornton laughed, Red realized the major was just joking, but it was too late, he could feel the color rising in his cheeks.

"I won't let you down, Major," Red affirmed, once his heart stopped fluttering.

"You'd better not, or Al's head will be on the chopping block," Major Jones said, and then dismissed them.

The first several weeks, Thornton familiarized Red with the camp, its rules and routines, and introduced him to the men who weren't out on a scout, due to a recent report of Indian activity some thirty miles from camp. The men were friendly toward him, but Red sensed they felt he was too young to handle the dangers one encountered in this line of work and they were reticent to put their lives in his hands. He often felt ill at ease when Thornton wasn't around so he tried to think up ways to prove himself to the men.

One evening when they were sitting around the campfire, one of the young Rangers asked Red why he wore such a fancy gun and holster since he obviously had never used it. When Thornton saw Red's body tighten at the question, he whispered to him that he ought to enlighten the fellow. Although Red didn't want to appear to be bragging, he told the story of the killing of the Old Man and his pursuit of the two men who had done it.

"He was fourteen at the time," Thornton added when Red was done. "What did you do when you were fourteen?" he asked the fellow who had asked the question.

It was shortly after this that the other Rangers started calling him Red River Kid or Kid due to the story as well as his mop of red hair. While Red wasn't particularly fond of the nickname, he noticed that the men were becoming more willing to go out on the trail with him. Word of his hunting and tracking skills spread quickly as he spent more time on the trail with others, and for the first time in his life Red felt a participant in the camaraderie of a group.

Occasionally, when it was certain that the camp was safe and no Indians nearby, contests of marksmanship took place, even though bullets were considered too precious to waste. To that end, Red used his own money to order in extras with the supply shipments. With the exception of Thornton, he had beaten every man who had challenged him in a fast draw contest or target shooting, both rifle and pistol.

By the end of his second month, Red had taken messages to two of the other camps accompanied by Thornton. It was almost like being with the Old Man again since the Ranger was a fountain of information. Although he had already learned from one of the best about how to read sign and track, and even though much of what they discussed Red already knew, Al's insights on outlaws and on the dark side of man's behavior were invaluable. He learned that tracking a wild animal wasn't the same as tracking some outlaw on the run.

"It isn't enough just to know where the trail leads," the Ranger told him. "You have to think like a desperado. You have to know the location of water holes . . . when they're apt to be dry . . . as well as where you'll find settlements or lay-overs, like relay stations, trading posts. Places

127

where someone on the run might head to steal a fresh horse or restock his supplies. See, trailing a man it isn't merely a process of following along in a straight line. That way will take forever and you might just get yourself killed."

"That's what I did with those two who killed the Old Man . . . got out ahead of them," Red told Thornton.

Thornton smiled.

Late in June, Red was patrolling with Ranger Ed Halliway. They were a distance from camp, and Ed needed a farrier to check out his horse since it was favoring his right front leg. The Ranger hoped it was just a loose shoe, but with rumors of Indian activity rampant, he needed his horse to be in good condition. He knew there was a small settlement—called Twisted Gulch—not too far off the trail, so they headed in that direction.

While the horse was being checked over, Halliway suggested on wetting their whistle at the make-shift watering hole, the Busted Flush Saloon, more of a room than a saloon. Halliway wasn't as protective of Red as Thornton, so he didn't object to Red trying a beer. It was Red's first ever, and although he enjoyed the cold beverage, he still couldn't understand the strong attraction most men seemed to have for it. After a sip or two he concluded that beer wasn't anywhere near the best thing he'd ever tasted.

"It's an acquired taste," Halliway explained, chuckling when he saw Red make a face. "And it's more about the feelin' than the tastin', Kid."

An argument erupted across the room.

"You're a damned cheat!" cried out a short, stout man, seated at a table playing cards with three others.

"Just once," Halliway groused. "Just once I'd like to finish a cold beer without someone lousing it up."

Red said: "Go ahead and finish it. I'll take care of it."

The Ranger looked over at the table where two of the men were now standing as they argued. "You sure, Kid? They look pretty salty to me." He felt anything but comfortable letting Red handle it, but he decided to let him try.

Red had already surveyed the room when they walked in, but even so, as he walked toward the card players, he glanced around one more time. He also undid his holster's tie-down loop from his pistol's trigger.

"Hey, fellows, getting a bit loud, don't you think?" he said, as he approached.

The arguing men were leaning in and, not paying any attention to Red's question. One looked like a typical cowpoke. The other man wore a suit, looking very much the part of a card-sharp.

"Get lost, squirt, this don't concern you," the cowpoke said, without even looking at Red.

"Oh, but it does," Red said firmly. "Seems to me you're disturbing the peace. I'm a Texas Ranger, and my word goes here."

"I doubt that very much, sonny," said the cowboy, "but even if you are, it don't matter. I'm gonna give this cheatin' low-life what he deserves."

"Even if he deserves it, if you attempt to do anything, I'll have to stop you," Red informed him calmly. "Now, I don't want to shoot you, but I will if you force me."

"Like hell you will," the cowboy said, going for his pistol in anger.

Red's pistol was leveled and cocked before the cowboy cleared leather. Even though Halliway knew Red was fast, he was impressed, as he sat back, watching but ready.

"I'll take your sidearm now," Red said firmly. "Drop it on the table in front of you . . . gently . . . then take three steps back."

The cowboy's face paled and he quickly did as ordered.

"The cheat's been bottom d-dealing and d-daubing the c-cards," he stammered suddenly nervous.

Red had played cards with both the Old Man and Tom, and he had been told about daubing, a card-marking technique. Red wondered where the cardsharp was keeping the substance he was using to daub the cards.

The suited man stood up "I'm telling you, he's just a poor loser. Honest, Ranger, I don't cheat. I'm on a lucky streak is all." He smiled at Red, adding: "I'll just collect my winnings, if it's all right with you." He bent to gather up the money on the table.

Red stopped him, saying: "I'd like you to open your coat and then let me have a look inside both your sleeves." He had no idea what the cardsharp was using to daub the cards or where he was hiding it, but he wanted to scare him by letting him know he knew all about the cheater's trick.

The gambler hesitated and then slowly straightened back up. "Sure, Ranger, no problem."

As Red stepped closer, the man's right arm suddenly shot out and a knife appeared in his hand. Before he could react, the gambler's arm was wrapped tightly around Red's throat, and the knife was poised at his neck.

"Hold it right there dammit!" Ed Halliway yelled, drawing his pistol.

The gambler spun Red around, using him as a shield.

"I wouldn't try that. Drop the knife!" Halliway yelled as he walked straight to the table.

The gambler laughed. "Try it? Hell no, I'm doing it. I'm walking out of here and you won't stop me, unless you want the Rangers to be short one man." The gambler backed up a step, using his free hand to scoop the money off the table and into his outer coat pocket.

Ed Halliway leveled his big Walker Colt pistol and shook his head. "That's not the way it's going to play out."

As the two stared at each other, Red slowly slid his right foot backward till it was just inside the gambler's right leg. The outside of his boot was even with the inside of the gambler's shoe. Red shifted his neck slightly back from the gambler's arm, then raised his left hand to shoulder height, hoping to distract the gambler, remembering that Tom had told him that in a tense situation, a man has trouble concentrating easily on two things at once.

So, as the gambler warned him to put his arm down, Red cocked his Colt and fired right through the open bottom of his holster. The bullet traveled straight down into the gambler's foot, most likely shattering all the bones in the man's instep.

Just as Red had hoped, the pain caused the cardsharp to release Red as he fell back against the wall. Red backed away a step, drew his gun, spun it, and brought the pistol butt down heavily on top of the gambler's head. The man collapsed.

"That must have hurt," Ed said, holstering his own gun.

"The foot or the head?" Red asked.

Ed laughed. "Both I reckon, but he sure had it coming."

"You reckon?" Red said, shaking his head and rubbing his throat. He turned back to the cowpoke. "Am I going to have a problem with you?"

The man shook his head. "No, sir, Ranger, sir, not one bit."

"Good. Now since this fellow's actions told me he was in fact cheating, I'd advise you to take the money he pocketed that is yours, and then get back to your ranch job. That all right with you, Ed?"

"Sure," Halliway replied as he walked back to his mug and finished off his beer. "Let's go."

The barkeep pointed at the unconscious gambler. "What do we do with him, Ranger?" he asked.

Halliway went over to search the gambler. He found a hide-out revolver in a shoulder holster. "I'm taking the knife, along with this gun," he announced as he stood. Looking at the fellow behind the bar, he said: "I assume you've got somewhere to hold him once his foot is checked out. I'll let 'em know back at camp what happened. Somebody will be sent to get him. Let them decide what to do."

"But, Ranger," the barkeeper said, "the doc's out of town and won't be back for at least a week."

"Well, have somebody clean up and bandage his foot," Halliway told him. "And when he comes to, tell him the Texas Battalion don't take kindly to threatening one of its Rangers."

For weeks after the experience at the bar, while traveling between the camps, Red reflected on his narrow escape and how he could have avoided it. The more he thought about it, the more he became convinced that he needed to learn how to defend himself against a knife attack.

When he returned this day, he reported to Captain Barnes that he had cut the sign of a small group of unshod horses. When he was dismissed, he went in search of his mentor, Al Thornton.

He found the older man sitting on a tree stump outside of his tent, whittling with his pocket knife.

"Al, maybe you can help me," Red said. "See the thing is, I just can't help but feel that my experience with knives is lacking."

Thornton smiled up at the teenager and nodded. "Sure, Red, I'd be glad to help. Now, you need to try to make short, smooth cuts rather than sawing the wood back and forth. Don't try to take off too much. . . ."

"Wait," Red snapped. "No, Al, I'm not talking about whittling, and you damned well know it!"

"It ain't?" Al said, feigning ignorance.

"No it ain't! I'm sure by now Halliway has told

everyone in camp about what happened in that saloon at least three times."

Al nodded. "Yeah, I did hear that some no-account gambler got you by the short hairs. Ed said you got out of it all right. Said you stayed calm. Sure glad you didn't get hurt or . . ."

"Thanks, but I got lucky," Red said. "The thing is, Al, I wasn't even thinking about a knife when I went up to him. That knife seemed to come out of nowhere. Next thing I know it's shoved up against my neck. He'd have filleted me like a trout if it weren't for Ed pulling that big old Walker of his."

"So I'm guessing you'd like to learn how to protect yourself against a knife. I have to say that was smart thinking, shooting him in the foot like that. There are times when fast thinking is the most important thing you can do."

"Best weapon is your brain, right?" Red said, recalling one of the lessons Tom had given him. "So, can you help me?"

The Ranger hesitated a moment before replying. "Truth is, I hate going up against a knife," Al said, waving his pocket knife. "Red, you were right when you said you were lucky. The first thing you'll learn is that in a knife fight, you're bound to get cut no matter how adept or fast you are with a gun."

"So can you help me?" Red asked.

"Oh, hell no," Al answered. "I'm just as afraid

of a knife fight as you are. Other than telling you to keep as far away from a knife as possible, I can't help you."

Red was surprised by Al's admission, having expected a different response from someone so experienced.

Seeing the look on Red's face, Al told him: "Listen, there's this fellow from Mexico who brings supplies into the camps, mostly mules. Heard he's expected to be coming through any day now. He might be able to help you in that art. I expect he knows more than I do . . . has a scar on the side of his face from some fight he was in years ago. I reckon I might be able get him to show you a few things."

"Does he speak English?"

"Like a native, Red," Al said.

"So how soon before he gets here?"

The Ranger held up his hand. "Whoa, hoss! Slow down. I just told you he's due in camp, but I can't tell you any more than that. Besides, I don't know if he'd even be able to help you."

Red felt frustrated, but he knew he shouldn't get his hopes up. "Sorry, Al. And I'd appreciate any help you can be in talking with him."

"Sure thing, Red. I'll talk to him as soon as he arrives."

Three weeks went by, during which Red made his first trip to Camp C alone. Conditions at the camp C weren't good, the men tense. After delivering the message and having a quick meal, he hurried back to his camp, knowing Major Jones was expected any day.

It was a Thursday when he returned to camp, dog tired and hungry as an ox.

Red was busy brushing down his horse when Thornton approached him.

"Hey, rookie. After you get done here, come on over to my tent, there's something I want to tell you."

"Something up? I hope it's not another job. I'm beat," he said.

"Nope, nothing like that. My tent when you're done here," Thornton repeated.

It was nearly twenty minutes before Red stood before Al's tent. "So, what's this about?" Red asked.

"Let's get over to the mess hall, so you can eat," Al said, getting up off his cot.

"Good," Red said, brightening, "I'm starved."

They walked over to the tent where the food was served and a few tables were set up.

Once seated inside the tent, Al said: "Remember that Mexican fellow I told you about . . . Ernesto Astengo."

"He's here?" Red had trouble containing his excitement. "Ernesto . . . what? You never mentioned his name before."

"Astengo," Thornton told Red. "And yes, he's

here and willing to give you some tips. As soon as you get some food in your belly, he'll be over."

Red ate the warmed over beans and bread as though it was the first meal he'd had in weeks. Al couldn't help just sitting back and smiling at the speed with which the food disappeared from the plate.

"So where's Astengo? I'm done," Red said, using a rag that was sitting on the table to wipe his face and hands.

"He'll be here," Thornton assured him.

"All right," Red said. "What's with the secrecy?"

"Is none," Thornton told him.

So they sat there, waiting, Red's impatience growing, but finally a small man walked into the tent and they were introduced.

"I'll leave you two alone," Thornton announced, and left the tent.

"Tell me what happened," Astengo began, which Red did. "Now I want you to show me. Arrange the tables and chairs as they were in this watering hole. I will be the gambler."

Red did, and then he moved back, guessing the distance he had been from the table when the whole thing started. He walked over to Astengo, saying: "I was about here when I started talking to the gambler. . . ." Before he finished his sentence, the Mexican reached out and yanked him by his arm, turned him around, pulled him close, and had a knife against his neck just as the gambler had.

"What next?" the Mexican asked.

"I was afraid to try and pull his arm away so I shifted my foot so I could shoot his . . . straight down . . . through my holster," Red told him, his heart racing as if the incident was happening again.

Astengo kept the knife against his throat for a few seconds more before he released him. As he did, Red glanced at the knife in his hand. It was made of wood. Red flashed to the image of Thornton whittling in front of his tent. *Al made that for him,* Red thought to himself, not knowing whether to laugh or be mad.

"Sit," instructed Astengo. "In that situation, you were smart . . . how you handled it once the knife was at your throat. Where you were not so smart was getting too close to this man in the first place. He turned the tables on you quickly."

"So you're saying that there's nothing I could have done?" Red said in frustration.

"A knife can be even more dangerous than a gun," Astengo confirmed. "I could demonstrate that . . . show you that a knife is just as deadly and just as fast or even faster than a gun in the right circumstances. In contests, I have stabbed a side of beef over fifty times in thirty seconds."

Red's eyes widened in disbelief.

"The thing to remember when you are

139

approaching a man, any man, is that you must always be cautious. In this case, the cowhand was being loud and threatening, so you thought this gambler was harmless. You walked straight up to him. You got too close, and couldn't step out of his reach. Because he surprised you, you had to react. It is best to remain in control . . . better to act than react."

"So there is nothing you can teach me?" Red asked.

"We will go outside, and I will show you how to fight with a knife . . . what not to do, how to protect yourself from a fatal thrust. But the main thing you must remember is that in hand-to-hand battle with a knife, you must be willing to take the cut . . . because you surely will be, so you need to make sure it is not a fatal cut."

For the next three hours, they worked on moves, both offensive and defensive, and these maneuvers became more automatic and instinctual to Red the more they practiced. Then they sat around the campfire, discussing the art of knife fighting, and how Astengo had gotten the scar on his face. Although he knew he would never be the expert that Astengo was, by the time Red was heading off to bed, thinking about all that he had learned today, he felt better prepared to handle himself in a knife fight because he would not make the same rookie mistakes he had made in Twisted Gulch.

CHAPTER ELEVEN

It had been raining three days straight when Major John B. Jones arrived at the camp B again. He called Red and Thornton over to his tent after he was settled in and had received an update on goings-on in the area from Captain Barnes.

"Come on in," the Ranger commander said as the two men removed their rain slickers. "And don't shake those overcoats out in here. Leave them over by the entry." Jones waited as they shook the rain off. "Take a seat," he told them once they were ready. Now, Red, I want to tell you that I've spoken with Captain Barnes and he tells me you're a real asset to the battalion. I was pleased to hear that. And in light of what he's told me, I'm sending you out on a job with Thornton. Orders from Austin."

Red smiled, happy to spend some time with Al again and not just riding between the camps. But Thornton got a sour look on his face and groaned under his breath.

"Major, whenever you tell me you've got a job for me, I feel saddle sores starting to form."

The officer pulled a cigar out from a small wooden box on his desk and struck a match. After a few puffs, he nodded. "Well, Al, you're right. Plenty of riding is involved. But when isn't it in this work."

"Never, sir."

"This job it involves transporting a prisoner," the major informed them. "You know most of the men are out scouting. So I need you two to do it. You'll pick him up and then he'll be sent down to Houston to stand trial for murder and a number of train and stage robberies."

"And just where is this fellow now?" Al Thornton asked.

"He's at Fort . . ."

But Thornton didn't let him finish. "On the Brazos? That trip will take us right smack into the Injuns. That's a long trip . . . two, three weeks."

"Stop complaining, Al," Red said. "The trip will do you good. Help you work off some of that extra waist padding you're carrying." In reality it would have been hard to find a single ounce of fat on Ranger Al Thornton.

"Major, this young wise-ass here may not finish the trip. I might just shoot him myself," Al said sarcastically.

"You could try," Red said. "Major, who exactly is this *hombre* we're to bring back?"

Jones shuffled through some papers before he answered. When he found the one he was looking for, he glanced up at the two men, while he read. "Frank Lannigan. Believed to be in his early to mid-thirties, brown hair. Wanted for a series of stage robberies and . . ."

"Lannigan?" Al interrupted Jones. "Isn't he the one who killed that woman down around Houston?"

"Same one. Seems he robbed a stagecoach as it was pulling into town . . . which was pretty brazen. Something happened to his horse. The mayor's wife was leaving town in a buckboard, and she was alone. Lannigan jumped into her vehicle, and used her as cover to get away."

"I remember now," Al Thornton said grimly. "They later found the buckboard and the mayor's wife . . . dead."

"That's right," Major Jones said, shaking his head in disgust. "Did some awful things to her before unhitching the horse and taking off. He just left her there to die. Son-of-a-bitch discarded her. Stole a fresh horse and saddle from a ranch north of town. Then nobody saw him hide nor hair of him."

"How'd he get caught?" Red asked the major.

"He was attempting to rob another stage with a couple other men. Would have made a clean go of it, but the guard started firing at them. Downed Lannigan's horse. The throw knocked him unconscious, and then after the two scoundrels with him rode off, the driver and guard tied Lannigan up and took him to the fort along with the passengers."

"Seems like he don't have particularly good luck with horses," Thornton remarked. The major ignored the comment.

"So why was he taken to a fort?" Red asked. "These weren't military crimes."

"No place nearby to lock him up," Major Jones said. "The Army's agreed to hold him for us."

"Nice of them to help out," Al remarked sarcastically. "Don't suppose they could have spared a detail to escort him back to Houston so we wouldn't have to make the trip?"

"No such luck," the major said. "Apparently the fort's short-handed as it is with recent trouble with the Indians. Once we get Lannigan here, we'll have to get him down to Houston."

Ranger Thornton groaned. "Can we at least wait till the rain lets up?"

The major shook his head. "You leave as soon as you can be ready. And that better be fast. You won't have to take an extra horse. You can get one at the fort."

The two left the tent, Thornton complaining the whole time they walked to their tents. Within an hour, they were loading supplies onto their horses and heading out.

It was five days of hard riding before the rain let up. Red had never been bothered by rain and found constantly complaining about it didn't make it better. He had learned long ago that

144

Nature was not under man's control, and you just had to wait it out because eventually it would change. On the upside, after a couple years of drought, they wouldn't have to worry about finding water.

Thornton, on the other hand, felt no compunction about railing against the elements. "I'll bet the major did this to us on purpose," he groused. "Probably volunteered us for this stupid mission to get Lannigan once he knew the rain was coming."

"Yeah, like he can really predict the weather," Red said, grinning. "And since when is bringing in a murderer a stupid mission?"

Al brushed the rain from his beard, shifted his hat, dislodging the water that had settled in its brim. "Well, you know what I mean," he replied sheepishly.

"Don't worry, pardner, it's letting up," Red observed, as he studied the clouds up ahead.

"Oh, so now you can predict the weather, too?" Al sneered.

"I've got eyes, Al," Red replied. "Look up ahead. The clouds are breaking up and the sky's brightening."

"Yeah, maybe, but . . . ," the old Ranger stopped midsentence, and stood up in his stirrups, peering at the hills ahead. He squinted as he leaned forward.

"What is it, Al?" Red asked. He saw the

concern in the set of Al's jaw and he knew from riding patrol with him never to doubt his riding companion's abilities on the trail.

"Maybe these old eyes ain't what they used to be, but looks to me like there's riders topping the hill."

Red studied the area where Al was pointing. His expression became grim. "Al, I think it would be wise to seek cover. And quick. We're out in the open here."

The pair rode hard and fast toward a nearby gully that was deep enough to provide cover for themselves and their animals. They made it to the gully without being seen and tethered the animals to a small stand of scrub brush. The pair pulled their rifles from the saddle scabbards and positioned themselves belly down along the gully's incline.

"You bring the eyeglass, Red?" Al asked.

"Don't need it," Red replied. "It's a party of Kiowas."

"Hunting?" Al asked, even though he was already reasonably sure of the answer.

Red shook his head. "Doubt it. It's a war party if I ever saw one."

"Am I imagining things or are they coming from the general direction of the fort?" Al said.

"Seems like it to me," Red replied, quietly studying the band. "They're gonna pass us pretty far out."

Al scratched his beard and shook his head. "Not like them to go near soldiers if they can avoid it."

"You know, Al, I was thinking the same thing. It does seem a mite strange."

"Strange or not, I don't like it. They don't pay us enough to go up against those kinds of numbers."

Red didn't believe his friend for a moment. He wondered what had been bothering Al of late, because since he had met him, Al had changed and become quite the complainer. Still, Red had never known anyone with as much grit as Al Thornton, unless of course it was Tom Harrison.

"Nope, they don't," Red agreed. "But they pay us to do a job and that's what we're gonna do."

"You mean you still want to go on even after seeing that?"

"That's our job, Al."

"You know, Red, you are one stubborn little cayuse."

"Nah, a cayuse'd have more sense," Red joked, trying to make light of their situation. "Looks like the band didn't see us."

"And iffen there's another band right behind 'em?" Al asked.

"Well, then it'll be like the story of two men being chased by the bear," Red replied. "One's just gotta be a faster runner than his pard."

"I'm the other man, I suppose," Al said, smiling, before getting serious again. "I think those Kiowas are far enough out for us to go. Let's hope that's the last of them until we get to the fort."

For the remainder of the trip they stuck to their trail routine, but they were more alert for any sign of Indians than they had been before, forsaking even a small fire when they camped at night. Al rode out ahead while Red fanned out behind, zigzagging east and west as a look-out to the rear.

CHAPTER TWELVE

In the afternoon of the sixteenth day the fort appeared in the distance. Both men instinctively checked their guns. Something didn't feel right to them.

"It's awful quiet," Al commented.

Red pointed out some unshod horse tracks. "This doesn't look right to me."

"Me neither," Al replied, shaking his head. "You'd think you'd see some activity around the place." The fort was a combination of stone and wood buildings, but there wasn't a single sign of occupation.

"Let's go on in, but we'd better be cautious," Red recommended.

"Hell, I was born cautious, son," Al said grimly. "Let's ride."

As the pair approached the main building, someone from inside yelled: "Who goes there? Advance and be recognized."

"Hell's bells, soldier boy, we're already right here. How the hell are you gonna recognize us iffen we never met before? We're Rangers with the frontier battalion. Now let us in!"

A voice from behind the sentry called out: "Let them in, Sergeant. I think we can handle them."

Inside, they were escorted to the post commander. As they were led, they noticed a number of soldiers had been wounded and were wrapped in dirty bandages. Both men wondered if they had battled with the party of Indians they had seen on the ride in.

A stocky but wan-looking man stood on the wooden steps leading up to his quarters. The Rangers dismounted and tied their horses to the nearby hitching rail.

Introductions were exchanged.

"So what happened, Captain Jensen?" Thornton asked.

"Kiowa attacks. We fought them on and off for two days before they retreated. It's been a hard time. We've been low on men and ammunition for over a month now. This didn't help."

"Any fatalities?" Thornton asked.

"We were lucky," Jensen replied, his hands shaky as he gestured for them to step up onto the porch.

To Red, Jensen smelled like he'd been drinking as he moved past him.

"We can stick around for the rest of the day, if that will put your mind at ease," Thornton said, having sensed the man's nervousness. "Besides, our horses could use a rest. We'll be needing some supplies and a horse for Lannigan. We're to take him back with us."

"Lannigan," the captain said gruffly.

At the mention of Lannigan's name several of the nearby soldiers cocked their rifles.

"Hey, what is this?" Red asked, alarmed by how jumpy the soldiers appeared to be. "I thought we were all on the same side here."

"Seems strange to us that so many lawmen would be coming for the same prisoner is all," the captain replied suspiciously.

"There's only two of us," Al said, puzzled.

"Now, yes," the captain replied. "But a sixteen, seventeen days ago, two U.S. marshals and three guards showed up to take custody of Lannigan. He's long gone. Good riddance to bad rubbish, I say."

"Wait a minute," Red said, glancing at Thornton. "We had specific orders that originated in Houston and then were sent on to Austin and the Rangers. No one else was called in, or at least none that we were made aware of. Something isn't right here, Captain."

"Just who were these marshals?" Al asked.

"Never saw them before, but they identified themselves as U.S. marshals, had badges, the right credentials as far as I was concerned," Jensen replied defensively.

Thornton let out a loud breath. "U.S. marshals, my eye," he said, exasperated by what the captain was telling them.

"I beg your pardon?" the fort commander said.

"Captain, about a six months ago two marshals

were ambushed over near the Arkansas border. When the bodies were discovered, their badges were missing. It stands to reason the men you met were imposters . . . probably the perpetrators of the killings. They must have been working with Lannigan and used those badges to get him out of here."

"You sure about that?" Jensen asked, suddenly looking concerned.

"I haven't heard of any marshal working up around here," Al Thornton assured him. "Why would two marshals just show up?"

"How do I know you aren't the ones posing as lawmen?" the captain asked.

"Does it matter? Lannigan's already gone, or have you forgotten?" Thornton said angrily, annoyed with the commander. "Didn't we just tell you about the two marshals that were killed. If we were outlaws, why would we tell you that?"

The commander cleared his throat. "Yes . . . um, that does make sense. Well, I'm sorry you men had to come all this way. I know it's a long trip."

"Captain," Red said, "our journey has just begun. And besides having a two-week head start, we now have . . . what? . . . six outlaws to track down. So, with or without your permission, we'll stay the night, rest our horses, resupply, and, if those Kiowas come back, we'll be here to help.

But then we'll head out and finish the job we set out to do."

By ten the following morning, Thornton and Red prepared to ride out in pursuit of Frank Lannigan and the five men with him. They gathered as much information as they could from those in the fort regarding descriptions of the outlaws and the direction they had taken when they left, even though they knew it wouldn't be that hard to track six men once they were on their trail.

Right before the Rangers left, one of the lieutenants drew them aside.

"The Kiowas have never been exactly friendly, but until this recent siege they've kept away from the fort here. Seems like something must have stirred them up, and it all started after the release of that man Lannigan. Think there might be a connection?"

"It's sure something to consider," Thornton replied. "Much obliged, Lieutenant. Stay safe. And thanks for the information."

The young officer saluted as the two Rangers rode out.

After three hours of hard riding, Al slowed his horse. "You know, Red, we've done everything the major asked of us. We went to the fort and it sure wasn't any fault of our own if Lannigan wasn't there. We maybe should head back and let them know about Lannigan, the attack on the fort, and that band we saw heading into the interior."

Red shook his head. "The way I see it, Al, the major's instructions were pretty clear. We have to go after this Lannigan and bring him in. Besides, I'm sure our men out scouting will come across that band . . . probably sooner than we could get back to camp."

Al leaned back in his saddle. "Have you stopped to consider what we're getting into? They've got a couple of weeks lead on us . . . six of them heading who knows where."

"I can't believe you're worried about your topknot?" Red said, once again wondering what was going on in Thornton's head to make him reluctant.

"I'm not," Thornton snapped.

"I'm as aggravated as you, Al," Red said, trying to ease the tension he sensed was growing between them. "We can lay this problem at Jensen's feet. The fort's run poorly, the grounds were a mess, the men looked slovenly, and I know I smelled liquor on Jensen. It's too bad Lannigan was taken there, but he was. Now it's our job to rectify the error." Red paused, before going on: "At least we have a lead on Lannigan, and it's a lot easier to find six men than one loner out here. Might find a fairly good trail to follow."

"Good trail? With you along, I can't imagine not finding their trail."

"Thank the Old Man for that, he was always teaching me something from the time I could walk and talk," Red commented.

"I do believe I would have liked to have met that old geezer," Al said after they had ridden for a while.

Red laughed. "I think you two would have gotten on real well."

"Maybe so. Maybe so," Al mused.

After a few days on the trail of Lannigan and his gang, Red couldn't help but notice how the two had settled into a rhythm on the trail, sensing what the other was thinking and watching out for each other. After picking up the gang's trail, he stopped worrying about Al and quit reminding himself that Al's skills out on the trail were as good or perhaps even better than his own.

"These tracks head west," Red observed on the fourth day out. "One of the six horses has shoes that have the heels built up. Another one has a loose front shoe and occasionally stumbles."

"Even my old eyes noticed that," Al agreed.

"One of the soldiers back at the fort reported that there was a tobiano pinto among those horses," Red recalled out loud. "Even if they make it into a town, they should be easy to track down."

"Easy that is, unless of course they're covering their back trail and planning to ambush us."

"Maybe, but there's no indication of it. Look at the way they're spacing out their horses and the speed at which they're riding. While they're not ambling along, they're not racing to get out of here, and they're not bunched up. I don't think they're expecting anyone to be following them yet," Red stated with some certainty.

"I deal with facts," Al said, "and I don't believe things always go the way you think they will. Life will teach you that as you get older."

"So we just keep following what trail signs we can find, then," Red replied.

"Until we can figure out where they're headed," Al said, "because based on their trail, I can't get inside their heads."

For the next few days the pair tracked the outlaw gang, which had shifted from a west to an east-southeast direction. As evening approached, the horses needed a rest as much as the riders, so they headed for a water hole they hoped had been replenished by the recent rain. It was hidden, surrounded by a small stand of oak scrub. They were in luck, and at the hole they dismounted and let the horses drink. Red decided to give the horses some extra grain, and got out the two feed bags from his saddlebags.

"Let 'em graze but don't over-grain 'em," Al cautioned. "With Kiowas roaming and Lannigan's group on the loose we may have to move out fast."

"You know, I never would have figured that out by myself, what with me being such a greenhorn and all," Red said.

"Just saying, better safe than sorry," Al retorted, when he was taking the saddle off his horse. He tied the reins to his saddle horn, got out his blanket, and threw it on the ground. He stretched out using the saddle seat as a pillow.

"More grass for him to graze over there," Red said, pointing to a green patch of grass fifteen feet away.

"Maybe so, but, as I said, this way I can grab rein and ride out in a hurry."

"You worry too much," Red said.

"Trouble is, you don't worry enough."

"If sleep will make you feel better, Al, I'll keep watch for a few hours while you rest those old bones of yours and then you can spell me," Red suggested.

"These old bones are gonna be rattling around when you're too old to stand up," Al said as he tipped his hat forward and closed his eyes. "Wake me in a couple of hours."

"You just rest those blue eyes of yours and don't fret none. Ranger Red is on the job."

"Heaven help us," Al muttered, smiling. He pulled his blanket up and rolled over.

CHAPTER THIRTEEN

Thornton spelled Red some four hours later. Although groggy and fighting off a craving for a hot cup of coffee, Al sat alert to any sign of trouble. Once the skies began to lighten, he took out his knife and whittled. At the crack of dawn he nudged his younger partner with his foot.

" 'Morning, pardner," Red said, sitting up and stretching.

Thornton walked over to the saddlebags to put away his knife. When he thought he heard something, he jerked and the knife slipped from his hand. As he bent over to pick it up, cursing himself for being clumsy, an arrow whistled right over his head.

Al dropped and made a forward roll which caused a sharp pain in his back, but still he came up with gun in hand. "Indians!" he shouted, then muttered to himself: "If I hadn't bent over, I'd've been hit for sure."

Red pulled his rifle from his saddle and ran at a crouch to the nearest rock. Arrows began flying into their camp. Red pulled one from the ground and quickly looked it over. "Kiowa" he said, tossing it over to Al.

"Well, they got us in a hell of a spot this time, that's certain. You fixed for bullets, Red?"

Red shook his head. "In my saddlebags. Doesn't matter though, there's way too many of them, Al. I don't think trying to shoot our way out of this would be the smartest move."

"No way we can outrun 'em. They'd cut us down before our horses got two feet," Al said.

"Not what I had in mind, either," Red said.

"What then? What in tarnation are you thinking?" Al asked.

"Follow my lead. And whatever you do, don't shoot . . . no matter what happens," Red snapped. Then he stood, leaving his rifle on the ground, and started speaking in Kiowa, a language Al didn't know.

"Why do you shoot at the son of Bear Slayer, friend of the Kiowa?" Red shouted, and then stepped out into the open with both of his hands held high. He swallowed hard as he waited for a response.

For a moment Al squeezed his eyes shut, expecting the arrows to come flying again. But when he opened them seconds later, Red was still upright.

Al raised his hands, stood up, and cautiously walked up next to Red, looking out at the horizon. "I know some Apache," he said to his partner, "but no Kiowa. What'd you say?"

"I'll explain later. Just keep that hogleg of yours holstered," Red said nervously. He addressed the man he believed to be the leader of this band.

"You know of my father. He was friend and family to the Kiowa. I am the son of Bear Slayer and my partner and I aren't here to fight you."

The tall thin warrior moved out and dismounted from his horse. He stood stockstill for a moment, then walked closer.

"I know this name . . . Bear Slayer. My grandfather spoke of him and how he once saved his life. But how do I know you are his son?"

Red sighed and relaxed his breathing. He took a slow step forward, and when nothing happened, he walked toward the Kiowa brave, stopping about ten feet away. The other warriors watched him carefully. Red shook his raised arms and then slowly moved them down so that he could unbutton his shirt. He pulled out the necklace with the three large bear claws given to him by the Old Man so long ago.

"Do you recognize this?" he asked. "Will this convince you I am telling the truth to my brothers? We mean you no harm and I know the Kiowa would never fear just two lone men."

A number of the braves moved closer so they could better see the necklace. The man who had done the talking walked up and reached out to touch the bear claws. Several members of the band were nodding and talking among themselves, their eyes occasionally meeting Red's. Thornton watched from fifteen feet back, not yet certain how this would turn out.

When the tall brave let go of the bear claws with a nod, Red smiled and extended his hands in a gesture of friendship. The brave took Red's hands in his own and nodded, saying: "You will come with us?"

"My friend does not speak your language," Red said, "so I will explain to him that we will ride with you to your camp so we may speak more. Maybe you will tell us why the Kiowas are making war with my people at the fort. Maybe we can help."

"I do not think white eyes can help, but we will talk."

"Bear Slayer helped once. Maybe his son can do the same," Red reminded him.

"We will see. Get your horses and come with us," the Kiowa leader said.

When Red explained to Al what had been said, the older Ranger stood in disbelief. "Ride alone into a Kiowa camp? Just the two of us? Are you touched in the head?"

"It's the only way, Al. You trust me, right? And they could have killed us already, if that was their intention."

Thornton nodded. "I hope you're right, and heaven help us iffen you ain't."

The next afternoon found the two Rangers riding into a large Kiowa encampment. Red estimated there were over a hundred large teepees, stretching in a circle around several campfires. Braves and women and children stared at them as they rode in. Several scrawny dogs barked and nipped at their horses' heels.

Red had learned from the Old Man that long ago the Kiowas migrated down from the Montana area, and that after settling in the southern plains became some of the best horsemen among the tribes. During their ride in, Red had found out that there were a couple of Real Dogs in the group, the most elite warriors of all the Kiowas.

The tall thin brave who led this band was known as Blue Arrow. He was the son of the current chief, a man named Beaded Shirt.

"Until we meet with the chief and while you are in our camp, you will hand over your weapons," Blue Arrow commanded when they dismounted.

"I expect to get these back when we leave, Blue Arrow," Red said firmly, unbuckling his holster and handing it over.

"If you leave," the Kiowa replied.

"I don't like this one bit," Al remarked out of the side of his mouth as he dismounted.

"Well, we're not dead yet," Red replied just as quietly, not yet convinced that Blue Arrow or anyone of the braves didn't know English. "If we keep our heads on right and don't appear hostile, we may get out of this in one piece."

Blue Arrow pointed to a nearby tent, indicating that the two men were to go inside. The teepee had several large drawings of dogs chasing a deer. Red had no idea if they had any special significance other than decoration, but he studied the artistry as they neared the tent and then went through the teepee's tent flap. They both stood inside, looking around, before sitting on the ground, alone but for each other.

"These Kiowa tents seem larger than ones I've been in before," Al said.

"Let's keep our voices down." Red leaned in, asking quietly: "Did you see the large brave who came out of the teepee as we were heading inside?"

Al nodded. "Couldn't miss him. Tall as I am . . . and his muscles . . . twice the size of most men's. Built like a grizzly bear."

"When he opened the flap, I swear I saw a white woman inside."

"How could you even see inside . . . look how dark it is in here. Are you certain she was white just from a quick glance?" Al asked.

"Well, didn't look like she was dressed in Kiowa garb, and for another it looked like her mouth was covered," Red said. "Or at least I think so."

"Could she be from that Ellis group that went missing a short time back?" Al said.

"I don't know who . . . ?"

"Back at the fort, I heard some talk that a couple of wagons headed up by some fellow named Ellis was late in arriving," Al explained. "They were supposed to be heading farther west and were due to stop over at the fort on the way. Old friends of Captain Jensen . . . from the East."

Red nodded. "I suppose it could be. For now, let's just take it one step at a time," Red cautioned.

The old Ranger shook his shoulders. "Yeah, good luck with that."

CHAPTER FOURTEEN

The few times Red stuck his head out of the teepee flap, he was pushed back inside by one of the two braves guarding the opening.

"Guess they don't want us wandering around," Red remarked. "But I'd like to find out if I'm right about a white woman being in that teepee."

"Guess we'll find out about that soon enough," Al said.

About an hour later the flap was pulled open and Blue Arrow leaned in, indicating for them to follow him. They were ushered over to the center of the camp where a group of tribe elders were gathered. They were then instructed to stand facing the group.

After a brief conversation between Blue Arrow and Beaded Shirt, the Kiowa chief finally spoke.

"Blue Arrow tells me you know our language," the chief said. "That is good, so we will talk in Kiowa."

"I do, and proudly so," Red replied.

"He also says you claim to be the son of Bear Slayer."

This time Red merely nodded.

"How do we know this to be true?" the chief asked.

Again Red opened his shirt and took out the

necklace from around his neck, but this time he removed it and held it out.

At the sight of the necklace several of the Kiowas nodded, while others looked fearful.

"It was given to me by my father," Red told the chief. "He was killed a few years back."

Beaded Shirt reached under his shirt and pulled out a necklace. Even at a glance, Red could tell they were practically identical.

The older man nodded and smiled. "I remember your father. I was young boy. He was good man, good friend of the Kiowa."

"He often spoke fondly of his time with the People," Red told him, as he put the necklace back on. He left it hanging outside his shirt as a reminder of who he was.

"My friend and I mean you no harm. But we are wondering why the People are making war on the white eyes . . . why they attacked the fort. Why there have been more attacks."

"No peace now," Beaded Shirt replied firmly.

"What has changed?" Red said.

The elders began shifting as they sat. Red could tell that something had them agitated.

"We thought the soldiers had taken one of our women . . . Shining Star, daughter of my brother . . . to the fort. We learned it was not true. She was found dead. She was . . . dishonored . . . by the one who killed her."

Red quietly translated for Al.

"One guess who's responsible," Al said angrily. Red gave Al a warning glance not wanting to upset the chief. "Ask him when this all took place," Al suggested.

Red translated as the chief replied. Al stroked his beard as he thought. "The time frame fits," Red told him. I'd stake my life it's all the fault of Lannigan and his gang."

"We are tracking some very bad men. We think this gang is the same one who took Shining Star," Red told Beaded Shirt. "If it is the same men, they also attacked one of our own women. My friend and I were on the trail of these badmen . . . to bring these outlaws to justice when Blue Arrow found us. Great Chief, it will only cause harm to the People if you attack forts, no matter the reason. These men are the enemies of both the People and the white eyes, including me and Al here."

"Why is it the work of you men to find them?" one of the elders asked.

Here it comes, Red thought. He hesitated before answering but knew how much the Kiowas valued the truth. "My partner and I are Rangers," he said.

Angry murmuring began among the council men as they shot hostile looks at the two white eyes. The Kiowas knew who the Rangers were. They had fought them many times over the years over the home land. The white eyes moved across their ground with their cattle and farms, pushing the Kiowas back, pursuing them. And the Texas Battalion had been formed to be even more aggressive in the pursuit of the Kiowas.

Beaded Shirt raised his hand and shouted to quiet his tribe members: "Son of Bear Slayer speaks truth when he could lie. We will listen."

Clearly worried, Thornton watched the council men as they talked. Red stood his ground, studying the faces of the Kiowa elders before saying: "Beaded Shirt is right. I have stated the truth because that is who we are and I know that the truth is important to the People. My friend and I want to catch these men and bring them to justice."

A brave sitting behind the elders, stepped forward and shook his fist. "This white eyes lies. These Rangers wish all the People dead. . . ."

"I'd be willing to stake my life that the men we are looking for did this to Shining Star," Red insisted. "Again I tell you that we were tracking them when Blue Arrow's group found us. When we catch them, they will be punished. Especially their leader."

"White man's justice," the brave said, spitting on the ground to emphasize his point.

"I tell you as the son of Bear Slayer," Red said firmly, "that when we leave here, and we catch up with these men and punish them, I promise I will come back and tell you it is so."

"If you leave here," Blue Arrow said again.

"That is for the elders to decide, not you, Blue Arrow," Beaded Shirt rebuked his son. "We will talk now."

Red and Al were escorted back to the teepee. As they walked, Red kept his eye on the teepee where he had seen the white woman. This time the flap of the teepee came open and stayed open, and he saw the woman clearly. She was not a young woman, but not old, either. She was sitting hunched over, looking defeated. Red nudged Al's arm and cocked his head in her direction.

In spite of what they had seen, neither man said anything inside the teepee while they waited for nearly an hour before they were taken back to the council.

"Bear Slayer was friend to my family and to the People," Beaded Shirt began. "We owe him a debt. This debt we will pay to his son. You are free to leave, but when you find these bad men, you must return to tell the People it is done."

Taking in a deep breath, Red decided to take a big risk and catch the elders off guard. "And the white woman you have captive . . . she will go with us," he said.

The reaction of the council men to whatever it was that Red said, sent shivers down Al's back and he looked at Red with fear in his eyes. "What happened? What did you say?" he whispered.

"Wait," Red whispered, barely moving his lips.

171

"She is property of Eagle Claw," said the huge Kiowa they had seen when they first were brought into camp.

Red hesitated a moment, taking a deep breath. "It is the sworn duty of a Ranger to protect our people. I have no choice in the matter. How did she come to be here?"

"We found her wandering when we returned from the fort," Blue Arrow insisted. "Eagle Claw had lost his woman many moons ago. He needed a woman to cook and to . . ."

"To be his slave," Red cut him off.

"She is lazy, but she belongs to Eagle Claw," the large Kiowa declared loudly.

Red was thinking fast. "I believe she belonged to a wagon train that was supposed to arrive at the fort. But it went missing. That wagon carried among its people a friend of the captain at the fort. And you know because you attacked the fort, the white eyes will want retribution. It will not go well for you. But if you surrender this woman to us, it might help."

"You act like chief, but you are a boy," Eagle Claw said, then he laughed.

"We will not leave without her," Red repeated, growing more stubborn.

Beaded Shirt spoke next. "You both made your argument. But you say yourself, Eagle Claw, that she is of no use. She is an extra mouth to feed. . . ."

"She eats little," Eagle Claw insisted.

"Of what use is she, if she starves," Beaded Shirt replied.

The elders looked to Eagle Claw for a response of some kind, but he remained silent for several minutes. Then suddenly he burst out: "I will fight the white eyes boy. The winner will decide if she stays or goes."

A loud cry went up from the nearby braves.

"What's happening?" Al asked nervously as those who had heard the challenge moved out into the center of the camp. "I don't like what I'm feeling here, Red. What's going on?"

Red, still stinging from Eagle Claw's insult of calling him a boy, told his partner: "I told them if they let us take the woman, the Army and the Rangers might go easier on them in seeking retribution. . . ."

"Dammit, Red," Al broke in, "what are you thinking? You know . . ."

"And if I beat Eagle Claw," Red interrupted, "we might be able to take the woman out of here."

Thornton scoured his face with his hands. "That fellow"—he glanced over at Eagle Claw and shook his head—"is going to kill you, Red."

Red stared into Al's eyes. "I can't leave her here. It's not in me. I'm going to fight him, Al. That's all there is to it."

His nervousness and fear growing, Al tried a different tact: "You can't change your mind? We just ride out of here . . . ," he said as Red turned and walked to the circle the braves were forming around Eagle Claw.

He unbuttoned his shirt and stepped into the center of the circle. He didn't want anything constricting his movement. One of the braves gestured for him to remove his boots. Finally he removed the bear-claw necklace and held it out for Al to come and take, which he did, saying: "Good luck, Red."

When an elder broke from the circle with two tomahawks, Red felt somewhat relieved, since unlike a knife, it only had one edge and the long handle might make it easier to take away. Still, he knew it was a dangerous weapon as it could both chop and be used to apply blunt force.

Red tried to recall everything he had learned about fighting with a blade from Astengo: *In a fight with a blade you will probably get cut, so you must not think in terms of a single cut. Small single cuts are bad, but usually not fatal. Protect your vital areas—neck, torso, groin— your organs. Remember, you can lose an arm and live, but not a heart or lung. You must accept that there will be pain in such a fight, but pain is Nature's way of telling you that you are still alive. Do not allow yourself to be distracted from your goal. Concentrate on your balance and stance. Do not cross your feet or retreat in a straight line*

as your opponent can charge and push you over.
Remember to breathe.

Red tested the weight of the tomahawk in his hand before facing Eagle Claw. At close range the man looked like his muscles had muscles. Red gritted his teeth to keep from biting his lips or tongue.

Although right-handed, Red hefted his toma-hawk in his left, the opposite of Eagle Claw, who held his weapon in a strong-side grip in his right. Red wanted his dominant hand free when and if the possibility arose for him to grab and immobilize the Kiowa's weapon, or better yet to wrench the weapon out of Eagle Claw's hand, even though that meant his weaker arm would be the one he would have to use to deflect the Kiowa's blows. Red knew that all this was theorizing, since he had never been in this kind of fight and was uncertain of Eagle Claw's skill, which didn't even take into account his size.

He glanced over at Al, surrounded now by a small circle of Kiowas no doubt intent on making sure he didn't try to do anything to help his friend.

At a signal from one of the elders, the two men circled each other, judging their reach and the reaction time of their opponent. Eagle Claw was overconfident, which was understandable given his adversary's youth and size, though Red was not short by any means.

"You will die now, white eyes boy," the Kiowa boasted, stepping in and swinging his hatchet back and forth several times. Each time, Red managed to circle away to the side while parrying the blows with his own tomahawk.

The big Kiowa tried a hard downward attack, but Red had anticipated it and grabbed the blade of his own hatchet with his right hand. He held the tomahawk and thrust it upward to meet the incoming blow. Instead of standing still and meeting brute force with force, however, just as soon as Eagle Claw's tomahawk struck his, Red turned it clockwise and pivoted while stepping back with his right foot. This motion caught the brave by surprise and threw him off balance.

The Kiowa brave stumbled to his left, but managed to hold onto his weapon. He regained his balance and then turned angrily to face the young Ranger.

As he charged Red, the young man knew enough not to kick out at the Indian since, in such a fight, a blow to the leg would be fatal, and he was well aware that a swinging tomahawk is much faster than a leg.

The men parried blows a few more times and then Eagle Claw rushed in and the two locked arms. It was becoming obvious to Red that he could not match the Kiowa's upper-arm strength, and he knew going to the ground with him would surely be lethal. He needed to sap the man's strength, and fast.

A memory flashed through his mind of when, back at camp, he had been kicked by a burro. It wasn't a hard kick, but the burro's hoof hit a place between Red's hip and his knee, on the outside of his thigh. Red recalled the intense pain.

Eagle Claw tried to force Red backward by sheer force, and it felt as though he was intent on snapping Red's back. Red pivoted inward and, using the blunt end of the tomahawk, swung wildly and as hard as he could in the direction of the Kiowa's thigh, hoping to find that weak spot. Upon impact, Eagle Claw let out a whoosh of air and grunted in pain as his right side nearly crumpled.

Immediately, Red freed his right hand and thrust it, fingers first, like a spear right into the brave's throat. Eagle Claw grabbed his neck while trying to take in air, as Red slammed the inside of his right foot into the Kiowa's shin. Next he grabbed the lower end of the Indian's tomahawk handle. By pulling it down and across at the same time he twisted his own hatchet to the left, he succeeded in wrenching the weapon from Eagle Claw's grasp.

Now with a tomahawk in each hand, Red stepped in and swung them both diagonally downward at the Kiowa's head. Before they struck, however, Red rotated the handles so the blows struck the blunt side of the weapons.

Eagle Claw dropped, face down, and Red pounced onto his back. Holding the left tomahawk horizontally across the Kiowa's neck and securing it with his right knee, he pushed the brave's face farther down into the dirt. Raising the weapon in his right hand, Red let out a war cry and then slammed it downward. The force of the swing drove the tomahawk's blade deep into the ground just inches from the Kiowa's head.

Al Thornton let out a sigh of relief.

"I will not kill one of my brothers," Red said loud enough for all to hear, "but I will claim my right as victor. The woman leaves with us."

Both Blue Arrow and Beaded Shirt were smiling. The elders had been released of having to make a decision between a debt of honor and the demands of one of their strongest warriors. They could save face. And thankfully, no Kiowa blood had been spilled.

Red helped Eagle Claw to his feet, dropped the two tomahawks, and then dusted the Kiowa off. In the Indian's native language, he spoke: "You are a strong and fearless warrior and I am honored to know you. It would have been a shame to have killed one so brave. I do not want a grudge to come between us."

"Bear Slayer taught you well," Eagle Claw said. "You are the first to best me in a fight and you did so honorably. It is agreed."

"Know this," Red said to the tribe, "I pledge my word that we will track down the animals who killed Shining Star and the white-eye woman. I swear to all of the People, I will do my best to bring him to justice or die trying. I swear this as the son of Bear Slayer."

There were nods and murmurs of approval through the camp.

There was considerable mumbling among those in the crowd, but finally, at Beaded Shirt's nod, Blue Arrow went into the tent where Red had seen the white woman. After a minute, he emerged leading the woman to the two Rangers. Her gag had been removed but her hands were still bound.

Thornton pushed angrily through the braves near him and walked over to the woman. She was clearly terrified.

"Relax, ma'am, I'm a Ranger. So's my partner over there. Don't be afraid now. We've obtained your safe release." He glanced around the camp and shrugged. "Well, your release at any rate." He untied her bound wrists, and she began to slump down. He reached for her, which made her recoil, but he repeated again that they were taking her to safety. She calmed enough, though her body remained tense, to walk over to where Red was standing with Al's help.

"Ma'am, this here is my partner," Al explained. "Like I said, he's a Ranger, too."

Now that he saw her up close, Red could see he had been right; she was in her late thirties.

"Honored, ma'am," he said, tipping his hat. "Just call me Red."

The woman just stared blankly. The image of a ragdoll with the stuffing removed—hollow cheeks, sunken eyes, boney wrists sticking out at the bottom of her sleeve hems—popped into Red's head.

He went over to Blue Arrow. The two exchanged words quietly. Blue Arrow turned and shouted an order to one of the braves. In a few minutes the Rangers' horses and weapons were returned to them, along with an extra horse for the woman.

"You're something, Red," Al said when he saw the third horse.

"Again, I promised him that I would bring word of Lannigan's demise, and added that if I couldn't keep my promise, I'd return and offer you up as a substitute sacrifice," Red said.

In light of their precarious situation, it took a brief moment for the old Ranger to realize Red was trying to break the tension. "That'll be the day," Thornton commented. "Seriously, how'd you manage this?"

"I told Blue Arrow, in exchange for one horse, when I returned with word of Lannigan, I would bring him five horses."

"Damn, son, you sure can come up with some

tall tales," Al said. "Now let's get out of here."

"Agreed," Red replied, letting out a sigh.

"Ma'am, we're going to leave now. Do you know how to ride?" Al asked, as he moved her so he could look into her face as he spoke.

At his question, she wrapped her arms around Al's middle.

Al didn't know quite what to do, so he said in a soothing voice: "You're free, ma'am, so we're taking you away from here. We'll help you. Take care of you till you're feeling better." The woman was crying now and shaking her head. "We have to clear out before these here Indians change their mind. You don't want to be left here, do you?" Al said.

At this, she nodded her head.

Now Red was the one who didn't understand. He was getting tired of Al's quiet approach, so he figured he'd try scaring her into leaving. "Ma'am, from what they said . . . these Kiowas are not happy with you. If there's no use for you here, they'll . . ."

"Stop it, Red," Al snapped. "No need to scare the wits out of her."

"I can ride," the woman said, so quietly neither man was sure she had spoken.

"You ride?" Red asked again.

"Yes," she whispered.

"All right. Let's get you out of here," Al said as he guided the woman over to the third horse and helped her mount. He then checked his own horse's cinch before mounting up.

"This way," Red said, leading them out at a walk. He felt strongly that as Bear Claw's son, he should show no fear, so he kept his back straight and refused to look back.

As for the woman they had saved, he didn't know what to think.

CHAPTER FIFTEEN

The three rode for almost four hours before Al called a halt.

"Red, we're gonna pull up at that small creek over yonder. She can't go any farther," he said, nodding toward the woman, whose name they had not yet learned.

Al helped the woman off the horse and made her sit down in the shade. Then he and Al began to set up camp. Red picketed the horses while Al got out the coffee pot and two tin cups from his saddlebags.

"I'll gather some firewood and we'll fix you up a nice cup of coffee, ma'am. It won't be very strong as we're rationing it, but it'll be warm and maybe help you feel better." The woman sat shivering while she watched the two Rangers go about their tasks.

When the coffee was ready, Al handed her a cup. "Here you go, ma'am," he said, and smiled at her as she took the battered tin cup in her shaky hands.

Red noticed that she appeared to be more trusting of Al, perhaps because he was older.

"Thank you," she said, after it had cooled enough for her to take a sip. "My n-n-name is Alice Wasserman."

The old Ranger removed his hat and gave a short bow, saying: "Again, my name is Al Thornton and the young Ranger over there is Red. But now, if you'll excuse me, it's likely to be a chilly night, so I'm going to go and help Red get some more firewood."

Before he left, the woman said: "Thank you, Mister Thornton. You're very kind."

Al actually blushed. He wasn't used to the company of a real lady. Oh, he had had experiences over the years with saloon girls and such, but this woman clearly wasn't cut from that mold.

"Wasn't much, ma'am," he said modestly. "We're just doing our job." He backed away slowly and then went over to where Red was taking the feedbag off his horse to put onto the third horse.

Red glanced up as Al approached, studying him. He had noticed Al's behavior had softened around the woman, and he grinned to himself.

"She better?" he asked.

"She is . . . I think. Name's Alice Wasserman," Al replied.

"She trusts you, Al."

"I hadn't noticed," Al lied, averting his eyes. "Red, mind your own business. I'm gonna get some more firewood."

"Go right ahead, Al, don't mind me. But we have to get her to a place of safety, so we can keep on Lannigan's trail. And we need to resupply."

As he wandered away, Al mumbled something Red couldn't quite make out. It reminded him of how the Old Man used to act when he felt uncomfortable, which made him grin again.

After a paltry dinner, the two Rangers tried to relax, but both had questions for Alice Wasserman they were afraid to ask.

"Ranger Thornton, perhaps Missus Wasserman would like to wash up down by the creek," Red suggested, once it was dark, thinking she might be more willing to talk if she was cleaned up.

Al looked at Red with anger and embarrassment, but he calmed when it looked like she almost smiled, something Red took as a good sign. Red knew it would take time for her to recover from her ordeal, whatever it had been, and that it was unlikely to be something she'd ever totally forget. Even so, Red observed that she was looking a little more at ease. At least he hoped so.

"If you think it's safe, I would like to wash up," the woman said.

Al retrieved his rifle from his saddle and gestured toward the creek. She got on her knees by the side of the creek and used the sandy gravel to scrub her face and neck. She used the hem of her dress to dry herself, and then the two walked back to the campfire. In the meantime, Red had added more water to the coffee and he handed her the watered-down brew.

"Um, ma'am," Red asked when she appeared to have finished the coffee, "do you think you could give us an idea of what happened to you . . . how you ended up alone?" He paused to assess her reaction to the question. "I know it must be painful, but it would sure help us . . . as Rangers . . . to know what happened to your wagon train."

Alice laced her fingers together and sighed. "All right," she said timidly, keeping her head down. "Where to start? Well, I come from a small town in northern Illinois called Wilmette. I was married there. My husband Henry Wasserman," she hesitated for a moment, "was a good man. He was the manager of the railroad station there."

At mention of her husband, Red noticed Al's body tense up.

"We had a good marriage, but, about three years ago, Henry collapsed with a heart attack. He was only fifty years old. He died two days later."

"Our condolences," Red said sincerely. Al nodded in agreement.

"So what brought you all the way out here from Illinois?" Red asked.

"We had very little savings. The railroad offered a small stipend for all the years Henry worked for them, but it was barely enough to live on day to day, much less for the remainder of my life. After a few months, I was forced to offer my services as a seamstress. Wilmette was a very nice place to live . . . right on Lake Michigan, but as the town grew, the cost of everything kept rising and I had a difficult time making ends meet, but I persevered as long as I could.

"Then about six months ago my brother wrote me from El Paso, where he had taken his family. Though I knew nothing about the town, I figured I would be better off close to the only family I have left. I thought, too, that my skills might be of use in a frontier town.

"The trip was long but uneventful until I left the train and joined a small wagon train heading west . . . just three wagons. A woman, Sandra Jacobs, was traveling west alone, her husband died on the journey, and she was glad to have my help with the wagon, the animals, and the camp chores."

"Where'd you learn to drive a team?" Al asked, when she paused.

"My father raised dairy cows and goats. I started driving a milk wagon when I was just ten years old."

Al knew she was at the hard part of her story, but they needed to know what had happened to the wagon train, so he asked: "Anybody named Ellis associated with any of the wagons?"

"No. Why?"

"Seems another wagon train went missing with a party named Ellis. Not your concern," Al assured her, hesitating to ask what the Rangers still needed to know, but he did anyway. "So what happened here in Texas?"

A haunted look entered her eyes as she began again. "It was midmorning when I heard rifle fire and an arrow struck our wagon cover. It all happened so fast. Somehow we managed to get down under the wagon bed. So Sandra had a rifle . . . she was shooting at the Indians who were attacking us. They got close . . . but they didn't go after us at first. There were seven of us women . . . no children with us. The next thing I knew Sandra was quiet . . . hit by an arrow . . . right in the . . ."

Alice Wasserman put a hand up to her mouth and sobbed before continuing. "It was horrible. I pretended to be dead. They took the scalps of some. . . . They rummaged through the wagons. Then they were gone," she stopped, shaking her head in disbelief. "It got so still . . . like they had never been there. I stayed under the wagon that night. I was afraid to sleep . . . but I think I did for a while." She took a deep breath. "The next morning"—she put her hands over her face—"I just ran. I couldn't stay there. Then a day or two later . . . I don't know for sure how long it was . . . some Indians came through. I don't know if they were the same ones, but they stopped. One rode up to me . . . grabbed me . . . and flung me over his horse like a sack of potatoes."

"His name is Blue Arrow," Red told her.

Alice nodded. "He . . . this Blue Arrow . . . took me to their camp. It took a couple of days to get there. He turned me over to this other Indian . . ."—she glanced over at Red—"he was so big. I was so scared. And I didn't understand what was happening or a word they said to me. I felt like I was in a dream. I just hoped they would kill me."

"I'm awful sorry," Al said. "How long ago did all this happen?"

"I was at the Indian camp . . . two, three days . . . so almost a week. Time went by so slowly. They were always shouting in my face, but I didn't know what they wanted of me. When they tried to make me move, I would just go limp . . . then they'd leave me alone. An old woman watched me night and day. She liked to spit at me. They tied me up at night, but during the day except when . . . it must have been when you came into camp. I tried to roll over and kick at the tent flap so you'd see me. But the old crone dragged my feet back. It was a miracle you knew I was there."

Red turned to his partner. "Al, we need to get her to a town. She'll need women's things . . . a place to stay for a while till she decides what she wants to do."

"Couldn't I just ride with you? Couldn't you take me to El Paso?" she asked. She sounded desperate.

"We can't go to El Paso. I wish we could, ma'am," Red told her, "but we've got a job to do that can't wait. It wouldn't be safe for you to travel with us, and besides, you'd slow us down. We're long overdue in catching the men who brought a lot of this on."

"I thought it was the Indians that were to blame. Aren't they the ones who attacked our wagon train?" she said, almost angrily.

"There's that, yes," Al explained. "But we're after a man and his gang. He did horrible things to a woman and then left her to die. And we believe they are also responsible for killing a squaw, which led to the Kiowas attacking a fort, and may even have had something to do with the attack on your wagon train. We have to get back on the trail of the gang, especially its leader. We've gotten mighty side-tracked and that just won't do."

"Things never seem to be a simple as you'd like, do they?" she reflected.

"No, ma'am, they don't. But we'll find a nice safe place with good folks to help you through this time," Red said, trying to be upbeat. "Al, let's check on the horses."

The two stood up, assuring the woman they'd be right back.

"Are you thinking what I'm thinking, Red?" Al asked, once they were out of earshot.

Red nodded. "Don't need a map to tell me the

best place to take her is Baker's Gap. Nearest, too."

Al scratched his chin and then combed his beard with his fingers.

"Soon as the sun rises, we head out."

CHAPTER SIXTEEN

"Seems like I ought to know the name of that town," Frank Lannigan said, thinking out loud. He and his gang of five had ridden hard the last couple of days and were looking for a place to light for a spell—rest the horses, buy a few supplies, and maybe even have a good time before heading farther north.

"It's Baker's Gap," a lanky man named Cajun Bill said, looking down upon the town from the hillside upon which they sat.

"You sure?" another of the gang asked. He was a short, stocky half-Mexican named Paco, whose weapon of choice was any kind of blade.

"Yep." Cajun Bill nodded. "Been there once."

"Lively place?" Lannigan asked.

"Was before they went and got themselves a new sheriff," Cajun Bill replied. "Heard he was a Ranger for a while. Think his name is Harrison. They say he don't tolerate any outlaws. Can tell you the town's grown some since last time I was here."

"Never heard of this Harrison," Whip, the fourth rider and a loud-mouth, said. He was the youngest of the group, and claimed to have gotten his name after nearly skinning off a man's back with a bullwhip. Lannigan didn't believe it.

The other two riders were the Simpson brothers, George and Elroy. The Simpson brothers were only in their mid-twenties but were already wanted for stagecoach robbery.

"So, what are we waiting for?" Paco asked. "Food, drinks, and warm women await us."

Lannigan nodded. "Sounds good to me. Let's go, boys."

It was early afternoon when the six men rode into town. Tom Harrison was just coming out of the barbershop. If they say there is such a thing as a sixth sense, Tom's kicked in immediately. The sheriff took one look at the trail-worn men and had a gut reaction to them. The amount of weaponry they were carrying wasn't meant for hunting.

Desperadoes. No honest person needs that much weaponry, the sheriff thought to himself, *that's for sure.*

The men hadn't noticed Tom when they rode by him, since there was nothing about his appearance to attract any attention. Tom always wore his badge under his vest, preferring not to draw attention to himself when strangers rode into town. As a rule he only flashed it when he needed to identify himself.

The six men rode on past and down the street until they came to the Broken Arrow saloon.

Of course that would be the first place they'd head for, the sheriff thought.

It wasn't a crime to ride into town or to have a drink, but, likewise, nothing said the sheriff couldn't look through his files for descriptions of Wanted men. The problem was, since Red had left and without extra help, all the sheriff's files had gradually become a disorganized mess because he never threw anything away. It would take some time to sift through them, Tom Harrison thought, walking toward his office.

Frank Lannigan and his men spent the next four hours in the saloon, drinking, playing cards, and flirting with the women in their style which meant making lewd comments whenever one walked past. By late in the afternoon hunger had set in and they got up and left in search of some place to eat. John, the barkeep, had suggested a small place three streets down. He had spent enough years behind the bar to recognize this type of men and he felt relief when they headed out. He had sent them to a restaurant near the Cattlemen's Hotel, hoping they would get tired after a big meal and just spend the night there, even though he didn't think they could afford it. Although the six men hadn't caused any trouble while in the saloon, he hoped they made a quick exit out of town in the morning. Like the sheriff, John had a bad feeling about these men, who seemed more feral than human.

The next morning found Sheriff Harrison in his office drinking a cup of black coffee, and cursing as he worked his way through the jumbled pile of papers looking for old Wanted posters. He hadn't gotten a good look at any of them, but he wanted to have the notices together so, once he had, or better yet gotten their names, he'd be ready to check. He wasn't sure that he would have any luck due to the fact that most of the posters simply listed names and vague descriptions such as "middle-aged man with a black mustache" or "tall and thin with a scar on his chin, mid-twenties." He knew it was easy to give yourself a new handle or cover up a chin scar by growing a beard. As he separated the posters out from the other paperwork, he shook his head because although some had photos or drawings, there were plenty with just descriptions that could match half the pop-ulation of Western men. Besides, Harrison was a careful man, knowing that on more than one occasion an innocent man had been lynched or imprisoned for a coincidental similarity to some nondescript Wanted poster. He never wanted to be responsible for something like that, which is why he kept all the Wanted posters that came through his office, which left him in his current situation of having to sort through a massive pile.

• • •

John, the barkeep, was disappointed the next day
when the six strangers showed up right around
noon. The only thing that made him feel any
better was that Sheriff Harrison seemed to be
keeping a close eye on the men, walking past the
saloon every half hour or so, a double-barreled,
side-by-side twelve-gauge express shotgun tucked
under his arm.

The barkeep wasn't the only one to notice the
presence of the lawman. Lannigan had spotted
him walking past the window of the saloon more
than once and it irked him that the law dog was
taking more than a passing interest in his gang.

While they stayed busy playing cards, the
sheriff entered the saloon and went up to the bar,
stood there facing out, to study the six men. In
spite of what he had taught Red about not looking
for trouble, he felt, in this case, he best make his
presence known. He walked over to their table
and asked: "You boys just passing through?"

"Just relaxing and enjoying the town's hos-
pitality is all," Lannigan replied, finding it
difficult to hold back a sneer. "Not sure yet just
how long we plan to stay, Sheriff." It was the first
time since their arrival that Lannigan got a good
look at Harrison out of the glare of the sunlight,
and as he sized him up, his stomach lurched. It
was the gray hair that had thrown him at first,
being that the incident had happened over twelve

years ago. But he was certain that it was this law dog, who had passed through his town and killed his two best friends. This changed his plans for pulling out of this town at the end of the day.

"Care to tell me your names?" Harrison asked.

"No reason to," Lannigan answered.

"All right, if that's the way you want to play it," Harrison said. "But this is a nice quiet place where folks don't like trouble. So you might be best off by just moving on. The sooner, the better," Sheriff Harrison said with a smile but with a threatening undertone.

"What trouble are we causing?" Cajun Bill asked. "Seems like you're the one looking for trouble here."

Tom smiled. "No one wants any trouble, and there won't be any once you boys skedaddle."

Frank Lannigan set his cards down and stared up into the lawman's face. "Understand this, Sheriff," he said, finding it difficult to keep his voice calm. "I'll decide when and if we leave. You might be the law here, but unless we do something illegal, I suggest you just leave us alone."

Tom knew better than take this to a head now with no one to back him up. "I'll be keeping an eye out for you."

Tom Harrison hefted the scatter-gun to his other arm and backed away from the table and then slowly exited the saloon.

"You want we should take him out, boss?" Cajun Bill asked.

Frank Lannigan rolled a cigarette deftly, having decided that Harrison would meet his end before they left town, that he would know why, and that it would be by his own hand. As he scratched his finger across the top of a match, he said: "No. This one's too smart to leave his back exposed. Besides, with that sawed-off shotgun of his we could end up losing a man or two." He finished his beer and slammed the empty glass on the table. "Elroy, go get us another round, will you?"

"We're running low on cash, boss," Elroy said as he returned with three beers, then went back to the bar to get the other three. "Fancy-looking bank in town, why don't we rob it?" Elroy suggested in a whisper as he sat back down.

"You always was the brains of the outfit," Lannigan mocked. "Was it that you couldn't pay for the beer that tipped you off to the idea?"

George laughed and tapped his brother, who had always been slow, on the top of his head.

"Fine, go ahead and laugh, but it don't mean we don't need cash," Elroy insisted, glaring at his brother.

Knowing they were all almost broke and that the way to control a gang like this was with money, Lannigan knew he had to squelch the idea of robbing the bank. Leaning forward, he said quietly: "What do we know about robbing a bank? We've never robbed one. It takes expertise to blow a safe and the right tools . . . you wanna find somebody in this here town to help us? I say we stick to what we know, and we'll hit up a stagecoach or a train as soon as we leave town. That's what we're good at."

The five men looked at Frank, not saying anything.

"You know Elroy might be right, boss," Paco said, sharpening one of his two small knives with a wet-stone he always carried in his pocket. "But we don't hit it at night, we hold it up during the day."

Frank tilted his chair back on its two back legs, thinking that although it was risky, it might not be a bad idea.

Elroy kept his eye on Frank and when the boss smiled, he elbowed his big brother, wondering if his idea might finally get some recognition from Lannigan, instead of always being the brunt of his jokes.

"We need to check out the bank," Frank said quietly, leaning in again. "Find out how many people work there. Whether or not they have a guard. Those kind of things. But we can't be obvious about it. And we'll need a good reason to be looking around when we go in. Besides, with that sheriff watching us like a hawk, we have to be smart about what we do. I think the six of us being together all the time is attracting way too much attention. The locals seem nervous when we pass them on the street. Paco and Elroy, I want you two to get out of town for a day or two. See if you can hunt us up some fresh meat. It's costing way too much to keep eating at the café. We'll meet you tonight, outside of town, where we've been camping. The rest of us'll split up and find out what we can so we can come up with a plan."

CHAPTER SEVENTEEN

After another day on the trail, the two Rangers and Alice came to a rest in a deep arroyo where a small water hole had sprung up. The area provided good shelter and there was ample grass for the horses to feed on. They decided to pitch camp and spend the night before moving on again. After the horses were ground-hitched on a patch of grass, Red went hunting for something fresh for dinner.

By the time Al had a fire started, Alice had fallen asleep. He retrieved his blanket and put it over her, watching her sleep for the next hour.

When she woke and became self-conscious, he started talking like she hadn't even been sleeping. "Three more days of riding like this and we should be in Baker's Gap I reckon." In truth, however, he was not anxious to say good bye to Alice Wasserman. He was drawn to her physically, as well as to her fortitude. He was experiencing feelings that were new to him.

"What's it like there?" Alice asked.

"Baker's Gap? Well, you'd be better off asking Red. He lived there for a couple of years."

"Where did he grow up?"

"Look around you. Prospector found him after

an Indian attack. He was just a baby . . . an infant. So the old guy raised him and they lived out in the open till he was in his teens," Al told her.

"So how did he end up in Baker's Gap?"

"Best you ask me, ma'am," Red said, returning to camp, carrying a scrawny-looking hare by its ears.

Alice jumped at the words directed harshly at her. "I'm sorry . . . I didn't mean to pry. I was just asking about Baker's Gap . . . and how you ended up there. . . ."

"My father got shot there, and the sheriff . . . ," Red started to explain.

"But I thought your parents were killed by Indians," Alice broke in.

Red shot the meanest look at Al he had ever given him.

"Sorry, Red. It just sort of popped out while we were talking," Al said, looking sheepish, but still he continued. "The man who raised Red got killed. So Red went after his killers and got them."

"Enough, Al," gritted Red.

"You must have been awfully young . . . I mean you still are," Alice commented.

"I was almost fifteen, ma'am, but there was nothing special about what I did. Ain't nothing heroic about having the man who raised you die and then killing the two men who caused his death. Especially when you have to listen to people tell the story like they were there," he finished, his gaze shifting to Al again.

"I don't imagine there is," Alice replied, shaking her head.

"Sorry, ma'am," Red said as the silence weighed on him heavily. "It's just a sore spot for me. Imagine always being reminded by other people about a terrible thing that happened to you when all you really want to do is forget it." The minute he had finished that sentence he realized the blunder he had made.

Alice cleared her throat before saying: "I wouldn't want to have to go through that, either. But I accept your apology even though there was no reason for it. Nonetheless, I still think your actions were heroic. You were heroic again . . . as was Al . . . in saving my life."

When neither Ranger said anything, Alice announced that she was making dinner, that it was the least she could do. Red got up to clean the rabbit, and Al just sat staring into the fire.

Conversation was minimal as they ate, but still they relished their first fresh meat on the trail.

"So, what made you become a Ranger, Al?" Alice asked when the silence had become almost unbearable for her.

Al leaned back, shaking his head. "It just sort of worked out that way I guess," he said, "because of my father. I was pretty young when my family came to Texas to settle. My father eventually got caught up in the whole Texas independence movement and ended up in Captain Karnes's Cavalry Company of the First Regiment of Volunteers. Then he helped train recruits about the time of the battle at San Jacinto under Captain Deaf Smith. He was wounded and sent home. I felt sorry for him 'cause sometimes when he talked about his days as a volunteer, he'd get this far-off look in his eyes, like he missed those days of glory. The stories Pa told me, especially about Smith, stuck with me, and I became a Ranger eventually."

"You should be proud of your father," Alice said. "What happened to him?"

"He passed, ma'am."

CHAPTER EIGHTEEN

Frank Lannigan and three of his gang had gathered again in the Broken Arrow. Paco and Elroy had been told to stay at the camp for the day while the rest of them worked on a plan. Lannigan glanced out the window and saw the sheriff looking in, which made him grit his teeth.

After sitting around, waiting, Cajun Bill burst out: "I'm gettin' tired of just sittin' around here. Can't we figure something out?"

"Can we all just shut up while I think," Frank hissed. "I've already told you we have to have a solid plan."

Frank settled deeper into his chair, and when Whip started to say something, Frank gave him a sullen look that told him to keep his mouth shut. Frank had been remembering and thinking about that day twelve years ago, when his best friends, Garrett and Fritz, were killed.

* * * * *

The three of them were in their early twenties with too much time on their hands. They got odd jobs during harvesting and branding time, but it never turned into full-time work. Garrett was a big, beefy guy. Fritz, almost frail and

207

timid, was raised in a strict German family that supported the Union. His pa took all his anger out on his son. It was Garrett who always came up with the shenanigans that had been taking a darker turn and was putting them under the watchful eye of the law. Though Frank had to admit he liked the excitement, he felt when they were getting into trouble, he dreamed of someday marrying Abigail Dickinson, the girl who had always ignored him until she seemed openly flirtatious at the last two dances he had attended. In fact, he had planned to invite her to the upcoming dance on Saturday night. When he told Garrett, his friend turned on him and started teasing him. And when, at the dance, he found out that Abigail was engaged to Harlan Thompson, he left with Garrett and got stumbling drunk. The two slept it off in the stable, and when he woke up, Garrett had hatched another idea. Frank knew it was stupid to go through with it, but in his hung-over state, with Garrett egging him on, he finally agreed it would make him feel better. They headed to the Dickinson's house on foot. When Abigail answered the door, Frank felt like he was going to throw up. When she hesitated to let them in, Garrett shoved past her and asked to speak to her father. She said he wasn't home, so Garrett asked to speak to her mother, and when she hesitated to answer, a look passed over his face that frightened Frank, for in it he saw evil. Garrett reached out for Abigail and yanked her close, her back facing him. She screamed. Garrett told Frank to come and get a kiss, that he deserved it after all these years of pining over the girl. Instead of telling Garrett to stop, the look of fear on Abigail's face excited him.

The next ten, fifteen minutes were a jumble in his mind. He grabbed her chin, forcing her lips into a rosebud that he brought to his mouth. She bit him. He bit back. Garrett was tugging at her dress. Fritz ran in from the back of the house, yelling at them to get the hell out, that somebody was coming. Fritz pulled Abigail away from Garrett. Frank ran into the kitchen, pressed his back against the wall inside the doorway. A stranger burst in through the front door and yelled at Garrett and Fritz to move, to let her go. The sound of scuffling. Crying from Abigail. The stranger shouted at Garrett and Fritz to get down on the floor. And then a shot echoed through the house.

Then another. Frank risked peeking out to get a look at the stranger, and he saw him.

* * * * *

"Frank!" George Simpson said, nudging Lannigan in the elbow, and shaking his head at Cajun Bill and Whip.

"What?" Lannigan said, rousing himself from his thoughts, trying to convince himself that that stranger had been Harrison.

"What the hell's going on with you? You were mumbling . . . 'It's gotta be him.' Have you even been listening to what we've been saying?"

"Sorry, didn't sleep well and I'm trying . . . What does it matter. What's so damned important, George?" Lannigan poured himself a shot from the bottle on the table, downed it, and then another, then he said: "Listen, Harrison is a by-the-book law dog, so we need to know his routine, who he's closest to . . . that kind of information."

"I was talking to some kid yesterday," George said, "and he told me the sheriff seems to cotton to the schoolteacher, some spinster."

"That's good to know," Lannigan said, keeping his voice down as the glimmer of an idea came to mind. "That's real good. So she's at the school a big part of the day. Gotta find out what time she's there exactly . . . when she leaves, where she lives. You handle that, George. We can use her to distract . . ."

"Wait a minute, boss," broke in George, "I thought we were hitting the bank. Why in hell do we need the schoolmarm for anything?"

Frank knew if they were going to rob the bank, they would have to take care of the sheriff because he was a man that would trail them to the gates of hell. Not to mention the others that were likely to be dogging his trail since he'd been busted out of the fort.

"We have to get rid of the sheriff or at least distract him so we have a chance to hold-up the bank," Frank said, leaning in so other customers wouldn't hear him.

"So we kill him," Whip said, a smirk on his face.

"And get the town in a panic?" Frank asked. "No, we want him distracted while we're cleaning out the bank, and then we get out of town. If he decides to come after us once we rob that bank, he won't have a chance . . . six to one not being odds in his favor."

"And if he gets a posse together?" George asked.

"That would take time," Frank argued. "Just let me figure out the details." He looked at each man individually. "So, let me think."

The last thing Lannigan wanted was a division among the gang, especially one that pitted him against the five others. He told George to go look for the kid that told him about the schoolmarm and try to learn as much as possible about her routine. He sat waiting with Cajun Bill and Whip.

"So what are we going to do about the sheriff," Cajun Bill asked Lannigan.

"I'm working on that."

"Well, you better have a good plan, 'cause like I said, he's supposed to be a fast draw," Cajun Bill said as he poured himself a shot. "The size of this town you'd think they'd have a deputy or two."

"Well, lucky for us they don't," Lannigan countered.

"Couldn't find the kid," George said when he came back to the saloon some twenty minutes later. "What'd you work out while I was gone?"

Frank scratched his neck as he looked around the room to make sure no one was listening. "I've been thinking that we need to get Harrison so angry he'll forget all his training and rush in bracing us all together. Angry men don't think things straight."

"So what would make him angry enough to come after us?" Cajun Bill asked.

"I'm working on that."

"Well don't take too much time," Whip said in a disgusted tone. "Sooner or later word's going to get out that we're here and we'll have

Rangers and marshals coming down on us like a hailstorm."

"You telling me what to do now, Whip?" Lannigan asked, leaning in close. "You want to run things from now on?"

Whip lifted his hands up in the air. He knew very well just how dangerous Lannigan could be when mad. "Hell no, boss, I'm just trying to help is all. You know, pointing things out."

"Well, when I want your opinion, I'll ask for it," Lannigan growled. He looked over at George. "Go get yourselves a round of beers. I'll be back in an hour or so. If Elroy and Paco get back, come find me. Otherwise, stay here and don't get in any mix-ups." He threw some coins on the table. "Use this if you run out."

"You got it, boss," Whip said as he took the money from the table.

Lannigan scooped up the bottle of red-eye from the table and headed for the livery barn. He knew the fellow who was in charge was a tippler, and he was hoping to loosen his tongue to learn as much as he could about the bank, the sheriff, and the schoolmarm.

Lannigan was gone for nearly an hour. When he returned to the saloon, he went straight to the bar and ordered a whiskey.

"Where'd you go, Frank?" George asked when Lannigan sat down at the table.

Lannigan looked up from his drink with a sinister grin. "I think I know how we'll pull this off. Got information from the liveryman . . . his lips get pretty loose when he's had a couple of snorts.

"First off, the bank. They have three guards . . . one inside and two outside, one on the roof of the bank and the other across the street. The manager is an older fellow, always there, but not a very tough guy. He's more likely to crawl under his desk than put up a fight. The safe they have is one the best around. So we'll have to see how things play out and whether or not we can get someone to open it for us. Let's hope they've got plenty of cash in the front of the bank. Best news is, they stay open till five on Friday . . . which is tomorrow.

"The kid you talked to, George, was right about Harrison and the schoolteacher."

"So?" Cajun Bill asked. "How's that help us?"

"This town runs like clockwork," Frank continued, feeling good about coming up with a way to pull everything off. "Everyone does the same thing the same way every day. The schoolteacher finishes her class, sends the kids on their way, and leaves an hour later. Same routine every day. So, around one tomorrow we bust that routine wide open."

"Sorry, boss, but still ain't following you. What does this schoolmarm have to do with the bank or Harrison?" George Simpson asked, lifting his hat to scratch his head.

Lannigan grinned. "If anything was to happen to Harrison's lady friend, this schoolteacher, who do you think he would blame? He'll come looking for us. And all we have to do is be waiting for him. Once he's taken care of, we hit the bank and then head out of town and into the night."

"When you say something is going to happen to this teacher, what do you mean?" Cajun Bill asked. It was what all three were wondering, especially since they had been drinking steadily while Lannigan was gone.

"All you boys have to do is be waiting in the alley a block down from the school. It's secluded that time of day. You take her down that alley, keep her quiet."

"We going to kill her?" Cajun Bill asked.

"No," Lannigan said, as images of Abigail, the woman in the buckboard, and the squaw flashed through his head. "No, not this time. We're just going to rough her up enough to get the sheriff's attention. One last thing, you boys are just backing me when we meet up with the sheriff. I get to shoot him, and I want him to know why."

"What are you talking about?" Whip said, looking bewildered.

"Never you mind. It's the way it's going down. No questions."

CHAPTER NINETEEN

Harriet Garland found the students to be unusually unruly as school began early Friday morning. Her head started to ache, so she gave them an early recess to use up their energy so she could get through the lesson she had been working on for days. While rather plain in most respects, one would not call the thirty-six-year-old unattractive. Why she had never married remained a mystery to most of the folks in Baker's Gap, but since reliable schoolteachers were hard to come by, the townspeople were happy that Miss Harriet could be relied upon.

Miss Harriet was thinking that she would never get through the day, when a glance at the clock showed class would be over in ten minutes. *I can finally go home,* she thought with relief. She reviewed what she wanted them to work on over the weekend, knowing ahead of time which students wouldn't even think about school until Monday morning.

"Oh, dear," she sighed as she began pushing in the desk chairs and tidying up. By the time she had the blackboard cleaned, she was exhausted and had to sit down as the throbbing in her head worsened. It was sheer willpower that allowed her to gather up her things and lock the door.

The sun glare made her flinch so she pulled her hat brim down lower over her forehead. Wanting nothing more than to rest in her room, she dreaded the walk home even though it wasn't far.

Harriet ran her fingers through her hair at the base of her neck as she broke out in a sweat even though she had barely walked a block. As her steps slowed, she feared she was coming down with an illness of some sort, and that she might have to call on Doc Burns over the weekend. But right now, she just wanted to make it home.

The school was on the far end of town, near the livery; there were no plankways for walking, and her shoes were stirring up a lot of dust as she shuffled toward the boarding house. As she passed the alleyway, she sensed the presence of someone, and the next thing she knew, a hand came around from behind and covered her mouth, preventing her from screaming. Then she was dragged back toward the alleyway.

As she tried to kick the man, a second appeared and scooped up her feet and then the two carried her deeper into the alley. She tried to twist and buck herself loose but it was no use as she merely depleted what little energy she had in her body.

"Keep hold of her," said a voice some distance back.

Miss Harriet's heart beat faster and it was becoming difficult to breathe. As she tried one last attempt to break free, she let out a scream which was met with a punch to the side of her head.

The liveryman, Dickens, was carrying two buckets of water over to the trough in the corral when he heard the scream. He stopped to listen, but there was nothing. Not sure if he had heard right, he picked up the buckets, but then thought better of it. He scurried to the stable where Charlie was working, a young boy who helped clean up a couple of times a week.

"Take Brownie, and go find the sheriff. Tell him to get over here real quick," he told the boy.

"Why . . . ?"

"No questions, Charlie, just go!" he snapped, and headed to the room in the back where he lived. He grabbed his shotgun and then went out back and hitched a horse to his small wagon and brought it out front where he stationed himself and waited for Harrison.

Miss Harriet, groggy from the punch, was thrown into the arms of yet another man. He grabbed her by the shoulders and shoved her up against the wall, her head banging into the wall. The man came in and out of focus as she shook her head in an attempt to clear her vision. As his face began to steady in her eyes, he pushed his knee into her stomach and grabbed her chin, making her lips pucker. As he stared, Miss Harriet felt he wasn't seeing her, that he was lost in some reverie, as a glimmer of a smile seemed to appear around his lips.

"You scream again, Abi— . . . ," he hissed, then stopped and smashed his lips on hers.

She turned her face and screamed again as he recoiled, a smudge of blood appearing on his lip from the cut on her cheek. Again he hit her, ordering the men with him to stay back as he shoved her to the ground and dropped down on top of her, straddling her stomach and pinning her arms with his knees. He warned her to shut up as her head turned from side to side as if she was telling herself this wasn't happening.

"There's someone coming, boss!" a man shouted. "We gotta get out of here."

Thwarted, Lannigan cursed the woman, spit at her, and punched her in the side of her head again before jumping up and following the other three out through the back of the alley.

"I heard a scream, Sheriff," Dickens told Harrison as the lawman brought his horse to an abrupt stop, kicking up a cloud of dust. "Maybe down the alley betwixt the old feed store and the laundry."

Harrison dropped from his horse and hurried down the street, Dickens following behind as he cursed himself for being too old and infirm to have done anything on his own. As the lawman neared the alleyway, he slowed his approach and pulled close to the wall. At the corner of the building, scatter-gun at the ready, he glanced down the alley. When he saw the skirt of a dress, but nothing else, he started down the narrow passageway, calling out to Dickens.

"Bring the wagon! Now!"

The first thing Harrison did was feel for a pulse. It was weak, but it was there. He pulled the sides of her bodice fabric together where it had been torn, before carefully lifting her up and carrying her to the wagon. Dickens let himself down from the wagon's seat as fast as he could and helped the sheriff slide her into the back. Harrison hoisted himself up and cradled her head in his lap, using his bandanna to dab the blood off her face.

The ride to Doc Burns's house seemed to take forever to Harrison, but Dickens was trying to avoid the bumps in the road so as not to jolt Miss Harriet around.

Arriving at the white-framed house, Dickens again helped Harrison move the schoolteacher, and then went ahead to open the door.

"Doc, we need you!" Dickens bellowed out.

"I'm coming," Doc Burns called back.

Harrison was already taking Miss Harriet into the room where the doctor treated patients.

"Miss Harriet, D-Doc. She was attacked," a

frazzled Dickens explained as the sheriff placed her carefully on the examining table.

As Eli Burns washed his hands in a water basin on a nearby table, he told Dickens to go up the stairs and call to Ethel, his wife. "Tell her to hurry."

Ethel, a short, stout woman, bustled into the room in less than a minute. Gasping, her hands came to her mouth as she saw the schoolteacher laid out on the table. "What's happened?" she asked as she brushed her hands on her apron.

"Get some water boiling, Ethel," her husband gave in response.

"Somebody beat her up as far as I can tell," the sheriff explained as he followed her out of the room to help. "Leastwise that's what it looks like. . . ."

"Who would do a terrible thing like that here in Baker's Gap?" Ethel asked as she shoved more wood in the cookstove.

"I think I have an idea," the lawman said more to himself than her.

As he set a pot of water next to the tea kettle already on the cookstove to heat, Ethel caught his eye, saying: "Then why aren't you out there getting him, Tom?"

"It's not a him . . . it's a them, and I don't think they're going anywhere for the time being. I want to make sure that Harriet's going to be all right first. There's a difference between battery and . . .

murder . . . ," his voice trailed off at sight of the look on Ethel's face as he said the last word.

"I'm going to go help, Eli. You stay here and let me know when the water's ready," Ethel said, having recovered from the shock of Harrison's words.

She shooed Dickens out of the room so that she and her husband could get Harriet out of her clothes to determine the extent of the injuries.

The liveryman made his way to the kitchen with the idea of finding a bottle of whiskey to help take the edge off his nerves. The first thing Harrison asked when he entered the room was whether or not Miss Harriet had regained consciousness.

"Not yet," Dickens answered, opening and closing cupboard doors.

"If you're looking for a drink," Harrison said, pointing, "over there."

"You think it was them fellas who come into town a couple days back?" Dickens questioned the lawman. "If you need help goin' after . . ."

"Thanks, Bob. I appreciate the offer, but I'm not going after them till I know how Harriet is. Besides, I'm trying to figure out just what scheme they have planned and how and why it includes Harriet. I'm outnumbered, and if they wanted me dead, they could have done it at any time. Don't make sense to me yet. So, while I'm trying to figure out what their scheme is, I hope they're wondering why I'm not coming after them."

"So what you're saying is, you didn't trust them from the beginning and anything that makes your odds in a fight with them better is all right by you," Dickens said. "You know one of them came to talk to me the other day. Said his name was Lannigan."

Harrison bobbed his head, and seeing the steam was starting to build up in the kettle, he grabbed a towel so he wouldn't burn his hand, picked up the kettle, and then headed to the treatment room. He knocked on the door, and entered when Ethel said it was all right for him to come in.

"Put it on the table over there," Ethel said, indicating where with a jerk of her head.

"How is she, Doc?" Tom asked.

"Took quite a beating. Maybe a couple of broke ribs and some nasty cuts on her face. Nothing life threatening though. Can't understand what kind of man would do something like this to a woman," he said, walking over to the basin and wetting a cloth which he handed to Ethel. She dabbed at the dried blood on Harriet's face, muttering to herself as she did so.

"Don't know when she'll come to and then whether or not she can identify her attacker," Doc Burns informed Harrison.

"I'm pretty sure I know who did this to her," the sheriff said, a look of concern on his face as he watched Ethel work. "I'll be leaving soon to go find them."

"Should I ask what you're planning?" Doc asked.

"Probably better off not knowing," Harrison said. "I'll be back later, but don't hesitate to get in touch if anything should . . ." He wouldn't let his mind think about it. "Thanks again, Doc, Ethel, for . . . you know." He left the room, knowing he had to act now before it got dark, or wait until morning.

He went into the kitchen, leaned back against the sink, and, hoping he could get a straight answer, asked Dickens: "When this Lannigan was talking with you, what did he want to know?"

Dickens looked scared and started to reach for the bottle of rye, but stopped himself. "He was asking about the school and about Miss Harriet. Couple of questions about the b-bank. . . ." Dickens' face went white. "I wasn't thinking, Sheriff . . . he kept pouring whiskey. . . . This is my fault, isn't it?"

"Bob, get a grip on yourself. I need your help. You can make up for any part you played in this," Tom said as he stepped up to the liveryman, thinking he understood what Lannigan's plan was. "Can I count on you, or not?" Dickens nodded his head. "I don't have my pistol, so I'm heading to the jail to get it. I figure Lannigan's got one of his men stationed outside, so I'm going to sneak out the back. I'm not sure where they are . . . could be waiting for word at the Broken Arrow. So, in about fifteen minutes, I want you to head over that way. See if you can find them, but don't say anything. Meet me at the back of the jail. Then get over to the bank and tell Reilly to close up tight and finally get out the word to keep the street clear of people around the jail and the bank."

"I hope I don't get so nervous I forget all you want me to do," Dickens said.

"You'll be fine." Harrison picked up his hat and settled it on his head. "I'm counting on you, Bob," he said, right before he slipped out the back door.

"Good luck, Sheriff."

After the attack on the schoolteacher, Lannigan ordered George to keep an eye out for Harrison over at the Doc's house while he and Cajun Bill returned to the Blue Arrow where Paco, Elroy, and Whip were waiting. That had been over an hour ago and there still was no sign of the sheriff.

"Can we at least have another beer while we wait?" Elroy asked in that whining tone of his.

"I told you one beer and you've had it," Frank snapped, trying to keep his voice soft. He could tell his men were getting restless and he knew that wasn't good. Glancing at the clock on the wall and seeing that it was 2:30, he said: "Let's head over toward the jail."

"What do you think Harrison is waiting for?" Whip asked as they started to get up.

"I don't know. Let's hope he didn't fall asleep," Frank answered.

The scrape of five sets of chair legs on the rough wooden floor made the other customers turn to see what was happening. A sign of relief went around the room as the five toughs left the saloon.

They had hardly made it halfway down the block when they heard running behind them. They turned as one to see George hurrying toward them.

"Where the hell have you been?" Frank hissed at George when he made it up to the group, red-faced and panting.

"Where you told me to be. Sheriff didn't leave the house, so I finally took off," he managed to get out with great difficulty.

Lannigan stood there, trying to figure out what the sheriff might be planning.

"You think you killed the schoolteacher? That punch you gave her . . . ," Whip asked.

"If I had, Harrison would have been looking for us long before this. Let's park ourselves on those benches over by the jailhouse. We'll wait fifteen minutes. Then we go in search of *him* instead."

CHAPTER TWENTY

Red, Al Thornton, and Alice Wasserman finally rode into Baker's Gap in midafternoon. They were tired, thirsty, and hungry from the long ride.

"I don't wish to be any more burden to the two of you than I already have," Alice said firmly, having noticed the side glances the two were giving each other as they entered the town. "Just take me to the hotel. . . . Wait. What am I thinking, I have no mon— . . ." She sighed. "I assume the bank is already closed."

"Stays open late on Friday. But we're not just dropping you off somewhere. Red knows the town," Al said. "What do you think, Red?"

"Ma'am, I think you can stay at the boarding house. As for money, don't worry about that right now. I think we should take you to Doc Burns and have him look at those burns on your wrists and check you over generally. You've been through quite an ordeal."

"I don't think that's necessary," Alice responded quietly.

"I agree with Red," Al said.

Alice remained silent for a moment. "If you wish. But I don't want to trouble them at home. . . ." What was really running through her mind was that the whole town would soon learn that she had been a captive of the Indians. The shame of that seemed unbearable.

"No bother," Red insisted. "Doc and his wife Ethel are used to people needing help all times, day and night. They've even got a bedroom set up for people on the mend . . . not that you're in need of a lot attention. Will you let us take you there? I know it would make both me and Al feel better. Trust me, Eli and Ethel Burns are the most generous folks I know."

Alice trembled, but she agreed.

As the trio headed in the direction of Doc's home, Red observed aloud: "Mighty quiet for a Friday."

Minutes later the three arrived at the two-story house surrounded by a white picket fence that was covered in decorative vines. They tied their horses to the hitching post out in front. Al dismounted and opened the fence gate, holding it open for Alice.

Red knew the door wouldn't be locked at this time of day, but he knocked firmly anyway.

Ethel opened the door, a smile bursting across her face as she recognized Red. She hugged him and kissed his cheek before letting go. "My goodness, Red, what a surprise. It's so good to see you!"

"You ever met Al Thornton, the sheriff's friend?" Red said, backing up, hoping neither of his companions would see the embarrassment in his cheeks caused by Ethel's overly affectionate greeting.

"I know the name, but . . . ," Ethel began. She took Al's hand and gave it a pat as she glanced at Alice.

"Pleased to meet you," Al said.

"And who might you be?" Ethel asked Alice, reaching out her hand.

"My name is Alice Wasserman."

Al could see hesitancy and embarrassment overwhelming Alice now that she was back in civilization. "The wagon train Missus Wasserman was in was attacked," he explained. "We need to have the doctor look her over. . . ."

"What happened to you, dear? You . . . ," Ethel asked, but stopped herself from saying anything further as Alice averted her eyes and seemed to shrink physically.

"We were thinking maybe she could spend the night here, and then tomorrow we can get her situated at the boarding house," Red suggested.

"We'll figure something out, Red," Ethel said. "It's been a horrible day. Miss Harriet was attacked by some men. Doc's taking care of her. . . ."

"What men?" Al and Red said at the same time.

"I don't know. They've been in town for a couple of days. I think I heard the name Lannigan. . . ."

Al and Red exchanged a quick look.

231

"But I'm not sure," said Ethel, becoming flustered.

Al checked his single-action revolver. "Where's Tom now? Where did he go?"

"You just missed him," Ethel sputtered. "Couldn't have been more than fifteen minutes ago. Bob Dickens was here with him. He said Tom needed to get his gun or something. Oh, I don't remember . . . I've been so worried about Miss Harriet." Tears formed in Ethel's eyes as she looked at the two Rangers as if it were all her fault.

"Let's try the sheriff's office, Al," Red said, checking his pistol. He looked at Alice, saying: "You stay here. We'll come back as soon as we can." He turned to the doctor's wife. "Do everything you can for her, Missus Burns. I'll be paying for Miss Harriet."

"Has to be Lannigan's gang," Al said, as the two hurried out the door to their horses.

"I'm gonna kill that S.O.B.," Red hissed, his eyes pinpoints of determination.

"Get in line, Red," Al said.

Taking the alleyway at the back of the buildings, Tom Harrison marched to his office like a demon possessed. Never before in his life had he ever been as angry and calm at the same time. Logic told him he should be scared, having to go up against six men, but he was past fear. In that moment he didn't care what happened to him, just as long as he had a chance to get Frank Lannigan.

Arriving at the back door of the jailhouse, he went inside, keeping away from the windows and making as little noise as possible. He buckled on his holster, loaded his gun with six bullets, placed it in its holster, and practiced drawing it several times. Leaving the same way he had come in, he put his hand on the knob, but then glanced back into the room as an image of Harriet's face flashed through his mind. He said a prayer for her as he closed the door softly behind him. He cocked his head at the sound of horses out on the main street, but they passed on by. He was waiting for less than five minutes when Dickens arrived.

"They're out front," Dickens told him. "Three on one side of the street, three on the other."

"Thanks, Bob. Now get the word out to stay clear of the blocks around here."

"Already did that," Dickens told him. "It's quiet out there."

Harrison patted Dickens, then moved down the alleyway so he could come out onto the street half a block down from where the men had positioned themselves.

He rounded the corner and saw them. Three were sitting on the bench in front of the building across from the jail and three were leaning against the hitching rail positioned between the jail and the building next door.

"Looking for me, Sheriff?" Lannigan called out, pushing himself up from the hitching rail, as did the two next to him.

Harrison kept his eyes on Lannigan, but out of the corner of his eye he could see that the three across the street had gotten up from the bench and were headed over to side Lannigan. He made no move as the six came together in a line in the middle of the street, shoulder to shoulder, facing him straight on.

It was certainly not how he had expected things to play out. After Dickens told him what Lannigan had wanted to know, he was pretty well convinced that the attack on Harriet was meant as a distraction in order to rob the bank, not as a way to draw him into a confrontation. But now he wasn't sure. But why would Lannigan want to provoke a confrontation with him?

He knew what such odds meant for him, that he didn't have a chance, but he would take out as many of them as he could before taking his last breath. This was his town and his job, and he intended to do the best he could, the right way—with honor—because he had taken an oath to serve and protect and to enforce the law. His word was his bond, and as far as Tom was concerned a man's sworn word was something that was in fact worth dying for.

"Saying it again . . . looking for me?" Lannigan said.

"It seems you're looking for me," Harrison replied.

"Well, well, well, if it isn't Sheriff Harrison, trying to act so innocent, and him being a killer of innocent men," declared Lannigan.

"I don't think you're a man I would call innocent, or your friends, either," the sheriff shot back.

"Wasn't talking about me," Lannigan hissed.

"Then I don't know what you're talking about," Harrison said, tiring of the game Lannigan seemed to be playing.

"How convenient for a by-the-book lawman," Lannigan said, laughing. He looked at his men, saying: "Ain't that convenient, boys?"

Harrison could see Lannigan's men had no idea what their boss was talking about either, even though they nodded, and one said: "Sure, boss."

"Are you telling me you don't remember passing through a small settlement about twelve years ago? Don't recall sticking your nose in where it didn't belong and killing two young men?" Lannigan stopped to let his words sink in.

"I don't know what you're talking about. Twelve years ago, I was a rancher, married, with a son."

"But you look just like the man that killed Garrett and Fritz . . . my two friends."

"You're dead wrong, Lannigan. You've mistaken me for someone else."

"You're a liar, Harrison. It was you!" Lannigan said, his voice getting louder with each word. "And that's why you're going to pay for those two murders today!"

Harrison could see the anger, maybe even some confusion, in the outlaw's face. "You would have been smart to have left town when I gave you the chance," Tom said, trying to throw him off even more. "Because now I have no choice but to arrest you for what you did to Miss Harriet. I'm sure you're wanted for plenty of other crimes as well. So, you can take your chances with me, or you can drop your weapons and raise your arms high over your heads."

The two Rangers rode their horses down the alleyway behind the main street buildings and toward the jail.

"Whoa, pull up, Red," Al cautioned raising his left arm.

"What's wrong, Al?" Red asked. "The office is just up ahead."

"I never was one for running full bore into a fight. There's six against one out there. I know three against that many are better odds, but we don't want Tom getting shot when we step into the mix. We can't go in blind."

"So what'd you have in mind Al?" Red asked.

236

"Let's tie our cayuses up here and have a look around the corner."

The two tied their horses to a post and moved to the corner. Red took a look down the street. Al looked, too. What they saw worried them—Tom Harrison was standing alone in the street facing a line of six armed outlaws, a good distance from where the two Rangers were positioned.

"He always was a mite too brave for my liking," Al said, shaking his head. "Now look what he's done and got himself into. What are we supposed to do now? We step out, all hell will break loose with Tom right in the middle." He looked over at his younger partner. "Any ideas? Remember we don't want to spook them into shooting."

Red's mind was racing. "We just need to buy enough time to reach Tom, right?" he finally said. "So I have an idea." Red ran back to the horses and freed the reins of his chocolate roan. When he walked the horse over, the creases on Al's brow became even more pronounced as he wondered what Red had in mind.

"You're not thinking of riding into that melee?" he asked.

"It would be like touching off a powder keg, if I rode in," Red said knowingly. "We just need to distract them long enough to move in. So I'm doing this." Red slapped his horse hard on its backside.

Startled, the roan took off running, right around the corner and down the street.

So far it had been a stand-off between Harrison and Lannigan's men. For the last two minutes no words had been spoken, no movement detected.

"You can see we're not dropping our weapons, Mister Lawman," one of the men said tauntingly. "So what say we get on with it."

It was precisely at that moment that a horse whinnied and came galloping around the corner from down the block. It was heading straight for the six startled outlaws.

As the chocolate roan passed Harrison, he recognized the animal and gave it a swat on the rump as it ran past. The horse balked and started kicking. Lannigan and his men were forced to jump aside as the animal veered from side to side. The sheriff started to smile as he heard the sound of running behind him and getting closer.

"Red . . . Al . . . 'bout time. How've you been?" Tom said when they were still feet behind him.

The two Rangers took up a position on either side of Tom, greeting their friend with a nod when the lawman glanced first at Red, then Al.

"Been real good, Tom," Red answered his mentor's question.

"Nice to see you, Al, but I have to admit your timing's a little off these days."

"Ain't no fun in arriving early. Better to get there just in the nick o' time," Al replied.

Once the roan had moved on, Lannigan saw two men flanking the sheriff, but he dismissed them, as his gang came together again.

"A snot-nosed kid and an old geezer don't rightly seem to even up the odds in your favor, Sheriff?" Still, in spite of his bluster, the outlaw didn't sound as confident as he had a few minutes earlier.

"Depends who the kid and the old geezer are, I suppose," Tom replied. "These two happen to be Rangers."

"We eat Rangers for breakfast, don't we, boys? And we like 'em best seasoned with a little lead in 'em," said the tall lanky man.

"I still count six of us to three of you. Pretty bad odds if you ask me, Sheriff," Lannigan said.

Harrison's eyes never shifted from the leader of this gang, and he could see the man was itching for this to be over.

The sheriff saw Lannigan's hand twitch and shift. Lannigan's shot went wild, coming as it did a second after Harrison had fired his gun. Harrison's bullet found its mark. Lannigan's bullet ricocheted and hit the sheriff in the arm, which threw him off balance.

As the sheriff turned, a bullet grazed his head, but he kept firing right along with Red and Thornton.

Those who were brave enough to watch the scene play out from positions of safety later reported that the gunfire from all those pistols seemed simultaneous. The bullets that hit Tom were fluke shots or ricocheting bullets, since everyone claimed not a one of the outlaws ever got their guns up and level. Two fired their guns as they fell, and it was probably one of those bullets that hit Al in the leg.

"Red," Harrison said, "are you O.K.?"

"I'm good, Tom," Red said as he tried to get Tom to move the bandanna he had pressed to his head, so he could get a look at the wound. "Al took a bullet to the leg . . . but you know it will take more than that to kill that old cuss."

Harrison let out a painful laugh.

"Dickens is bringing over a wagon to help get Al over to Doc Burns's house. Let's wait and go with him, get you checked out."

"It's nothing but a scratch," Tom assured him.

A few minutes later, Red heard the wagon coming, and relief washed over him even though he knew neither Tom nor Al's wounds were fatal. Still, it was going to be a long and busy night for Doc.

CHAPTER TWENTY-ONE

It was a long night for everybody. Conscious now, Harriet was staying in the room the Burns had set up years ago for patients. After being seen to by the doctor, Al and Tom were back at the sheriff's house. Alice Wasserman was given a room at the boarding house, but she hadn't stepped foot in it since all her time was spent at either the Burns's or the sheriff's house.

Luckily for both Al and Tom the bullets hadn't broken any bones, though at the angle the bullet had entered Al's thigh it had torn up the muscle pretty bad. Al said it was nothing and he'd be back on his two feet in no time. He also said that he hoped the bullet that grazed Tom's head would knock some sense into him. Red kept thinking how lucky Tom had been that they had shown up.

For Al, his wound had clarified what he'd been thinking for a number of months now. He was getting too old for this young man's work. There had been times during the shoot-out when he knew his timing was off and his vision just wasn't what it should be, especially considering it was daylight. So he was thinking it might be time to slow down. Now all he had to do was break the news to Red, which he knew would be harder than letting Major Jones know.

As the days passed, it was obvious to everyone that Harriet's convalescence would take far longer than either Al's or Tom's, though they were optimistic in their conversations about her. They had moved her bed into the parlor where the sunlight poured in, hoping it would boost her spirits. It seemed to have the opposite effect, serving only to make her burrow deeper under the covers. She barely ate and she rarely initiated a conversation, unless she needed something and then she would become emotional. A few of her students stopped in to wish her well, but they left within a few minutes, bewildered by her behavior and fearful that a new teacher would have to be found if she didn't get better.

Although they had endured similar, if not identical, experiences, Alice felt a kinship with Harriet. She spent long hours sitting with her during the day and into the wee hours of the night. Her attempts at conversation brought no response, so most of the time she just sat with her.

Red was making his presence known, patrolling the town at regular intervals so the townsfolk would feel someone was watching out for them while Tom was recovering. The slightest commotion appeared to set the town on edge. The women of Baker's Gap didn't feel safe since the attack upon Harriet, even though Dickens assured everybody that the men responsible were buried. He also reminded them that with two Rangers and a sheriff in town, even if two were currently incapacitated, any outlaw would think twice before causing trouble in Baker's Gap.

It was four days after the shoot-out. Red had slept out under the stars, feeling a need for some time alone to think. He woke up and went inside to make coffee and breakfast for Tom and Al as he had done since the shootings—the widows not wanting to disturb the convalescents in the morning, though they still brought over supper. When he walked inside, he was surprised to find Tom attempting to make coffee in spite of his sore arm and bandaged head.

"I've had enough of being flat on my back!" he shouted at Red, without turning around. "And I don't wanna hear no argument about it."

"That's fine, Tom. You were the one who said you got dizzy . . . ," Red tried to remind him.

"Well, I'm not dizzy now!" He was still yelling. "I need to do something useful. Besides, I'm sick of listening to Al's snoring."

"Me!" Al said. "You make enough noise to wake the dead."

"Enough you two," Red said, walking over to the table where Tom was trying to open the coffee tin. "Here, let me do that."

"Go to hell," Tom said as he handed the coffee to Red.

"You two are delightful to be around this fine morning," Red said.

"Why are you including me in this?" Al asked, sitting up. "Get me that stick, so I can get over to the table."

"Go to hell!" Tom repeated.

"I'm headed to the privy," Red said in desperation. "Work this out while I'm gone." He arched an eyebrow at them, slamming the door on the way out.

"Look what you've gone and done, Al." Tom stood staring at the door and then moved to help the Ranger maneuver over to a chair at the table. "I'm just angry with myself. Taking it out on the two of you. When . . ."

"You couldn't have known, Tom," Al said.

"I'm talking about years of experience being a lawman, Al. My instincts should have warned me. Should've had them locked up before they got off their horses."

"Lannigan was locked up and he got away," Al told him again for what seemed the hundredth time.

"To hell with it!" Tom shouted.

"With what?" Al asked, and then he and Tom started laughing and they were still laughing when Red opened the door.

"Glad you two worked it out," he said, smiling and shaking his head. "Now how about I make some breakfast. When Doc gets here, we'll have him take that head bandage off of you, Tom, and I'll take you over to see Harriet." He paused and put his hands up. "I know you haven't wanted to go because you didn't want her to see that you had gotten hurt, but she's not doing well."

Tom pulled a chair out and sat down at the table while Red poured out three cups of coffee. "What do you mean, Red . . . not doing well?"

"Doesn't talk. Barely eating. Stays in bed all the time. Alice sits with her a lot. She wasn't even cheered up when a couple of students stopped in."

"That's a real shame," Al commented, seeing the worry in Tom's eyes.

"Yes, it is," Red agreed.

"You're right I need to go see her," Tom said more to himself than the other two.

When Doc Burns checked in on Al and Tom, he removed the bandage from Tom's head. "The head wound looks good . . . no infection." He put a fresh bandage on Al's leg, who groused the entire time. Before leaving, he told Tom: "You're free to leave the house."

Half an hour later, Red and Tom were walking over to see Miss Harriet.

"You know I always looked out for Harriet," Tom told Red. "She never made friends easily. She knows 'most everybody in town, and everybody is friendly to her. But she just keeps to herself. That's why we had our Saturday night dinners."

"I think she has feelings for you, Tom."

"Go on with you," Tom said. "We're friends."

"She may want more from you, Tom. Remember, for a while, I was part of those Saturday night dinners. I saw the way she watched you."

"Bah and nonsense," Tom said as they reached the gate to the house.

The sheriff was either anxious to see Harriet or just being forgetful since he didn't bother to knock, but just walked right into the house.

Ethel peeked out the kitchen doorway, and shouted: "Tom!"

Red saw the embarrassment raising in Tom's cheeks, saying: "The sheriff wanted to thank you for all your help."

"The least we could do," she muttered as she came down the hall, wiping her hands on her apron. "Making a couple of pies right now."

Tom smiled, twisting his hat around by its brim, clearly nervous. "I wanted to check in on Miss Harriet while I was here, too."

"Go right in the parlor," she told him. "It's the brightest room in the house and we . . . Oh, listen to me carrying on. Just go right in."

Red started to follow, thinking he might be of help, when Ethel Burns tapped him on the arm.

"If it's not too much trouble, Red," she asked, "could you go out to the shed and fill the woodbox? Eli forgot to do it this morning. He got called over to the Callahans. She might be having her baby, though it seems to me to be a bit early. There I go again. . . ."

"No problem, Missus Burns. Just point me in the direction of the woodbox. By the way, did you see Alice this morning?"

"She ran to the general store. Then she was going over to see Tom and Mister Thornton," she said, then paused. "Guess she missed Tom, didn't she?" And she smiled.

Red chopped more wood than necessary because he didn't want Eli to have to do it with all the patients he was looking after. By the time he had filled the woodbox, taken it inside, and washed his hands, Tom was coming out of the parlor. He looked thoughtful, but he had a smile on his face.

Red moved aside as he came down the hall and walked into the kitchen.

"Ethel," the sheriff said, "Miss Harriet said she'd like a soft-boiled egg and a piece of bread."

"Land's sake . . . I'll get right to that," she exclaimed. "Guess you're just what she needed. You staying?"

"No, not now. But I'll be back later," Tom promised. "Let's go, Red."

As Tom carefully closed the door, Red was anxious to ask him if Miss Harriet had really asked for breakfast.

"Well, I guess it was me that suggested it," Tom said. "I told her if she ate something, I'd come back later today. She agreed, so I guess that sorta counts as asking. She looks mighty sad, but she did smile once. I think it's going to be a long journey back for her." He shook his head, adding: "I'm a bit tired."

"Let's go back home then," Red agreed as he closed the fence gate. "I've had something on my mind these past couple of days." Red didn't know if it was his place to bring this matter up, but now he had. "I'm worried about Al, too. I've worked plenty with him over the last months and I don't think his heart is in the job like it used to be. I guess I don't really know what he was like before, but . . . well, I mean . . . he's closer to sixty than fifty, right?"

"Not quite midway. I know you're looking out for him, but I'm not sure he'll ever quit being a Ranger. Can't picture him sticking in one place for long. But then again, you've spent more time with him than I have in years."

"I think he might need spectacles at least," Red mumbled to himself, wondering if he had made a mistake bringing up the subject after all.

When they entered the house, Alice was there, sitting on a chair she had moved closer to Al's bed. She and Al both seemed startled by their return.

Tom and Red said hello to Alice. She jumped up and told them she had just made some fresh coffee and they were welcome to some.

Red saw Tom bristle at the invitation since it was his house and his coffee.

"Thanks," he said gruffly, not even trying to hide his irritation.

"Oh, I'm sorry," Alice said as she jumped up from the chair. "Let me get it for you. I mean . . . it being your coffee." She stopped walking and turned to look Tom in the eye. "I'm so sorry . . . I don't know what I was thinking."

Al sat watching with a smile on his face. "Alice," he said, "you need to calm down."

When Al addressed her by her Christian name, Red and Tom exchanged a surprised glance. Slowly, a knowing smile passed over Red's face.

"Doesn't look like we're going have to worry about what we were just talking about," he said to Tom quietly.

Tom studied Red's face, not having any idea what he meant.

Two weeks later, Red was tying his bedroll onto his saddle outside the jailhouse. Tom, who was spending a couple of days in the office, stood on the walkway watching him. They both turned when they heard a wagon coming down the street. It was Dickens's hand, Charlie, driving Al up in the livery buckboard. Red helped Al down, and then all three just stood there feeling uncomfortable.

Neither one of the older men wanted Red to leave, but he had to get back to B camp. But first, he intended to find Beaded Shirt's Kiowas and let them know that the men responsible for Shining Star's death had been taken care of.

Tom was thinking it was going to get lonely again, since Al planned on leaving too, once his leg could handle travel. He had decided to escort Alice down to El Paso, via stagecoach no less. Then . . . who knew.

"Give my regards to Major Jones next time he comes into camp," Al said. "Let him know it was time I take care of this old bag of bones."

"I will," Red promised. "And, Tom, you let Miss Harriet know that I'm still studying history every chance I get, and that she should get back to what she was put on this earth for."

"It's a promise," Tom said, nodding. "She is getting a little better, don't you think?"

"She is when you show up, Tom," Red said. "Remember that." He turned to shake Al's hand. But Tom would have none of that, and he gave Red a hug.

Red gave his horse a looking over.

"That roan of yours is in top shape and has sure served you well," Tom commented.

"That it has," Red said, smiling as he saw Dickens coming down the street leading five horses. He knew he was in for an earful now.

"What the devil . . . ?" Al squawked. "Red, you're not thinking of going back to them Kiowas?"

"I gave my word, Al. Told them I would let them know what happened with Lannigan and I promised them five horses. Far as I'm concerned a promise is a promise, regardless of who you give it to."

"Did it ever occur to you that they might have changed their mind about you since you left their camp?" Al pointed out.

Red shook his head. "Doesn't matter. A man's got to honor his word. You both taught me that. Otherwise, there's nothing or nobody we can trust."

"Even if it means losing your scalp?" Al asked.

"I gave my word," Red repeated adamantly.

"So you are going to ride all the way back to the Kiowa camp, trailing five horses," Tom said. "You do realize this is just you being stubborn again. Set in your ways like always. Why won't you ever let anyone talk you out of anything once you make up your mind?"

"Well, you know Tom, it's hard to change who you really are," Red said, mounting up. "Same reason you were willing to brace six men all by yourself. Don't worry, Tom, I'll be back."

Tom and Al stood there looking up at Red. Both knew there was no changing his mind.

Red took the rope that was attached to the five horses from Dickens.

"Oh, Tom, I almost forgot. I was thinking that if there are any rewards for Lannigan or any of the others, maybe it could go to Miss Harriet?"

"Way ahead of ya, Ranger." The sheriff smiled. "I've already contacted the authorities."

Red smiled and raised his hand up in a farewell salute. Tom helped Al up into the buckboard.

"See you back at the house," Tom told Al as the buckboard started down the street.

The sheriff watched Red ride out of town until he was just a shimmery shape in the bright morning light. Tom recalled hearing about the first time Red had ridden out of town. No one could talk that young boy out of his mission back then, and, now that he was older, he was even more set in his ways. The sheriff shrugged, confident that Red could take care of himself.

The lawman shook his head. He gave one last look down the street before entering his office, thinking to himself: *Godspeed, son.*

ABOUT THE AUTHOR

R. W. Stone inherited his love for Western adventure from his father, a former Army Air Corps armaments officer and horse enthusiast. He taught his son both to ride and shoot at a very early age. Many of those who grew up in the late 1950s and early 1960s remember it as a time before urban sprawl, when Westerns dominated both television and the cinema, and Stone began writing later in life in an attempt to recapture some of that past spirit he had enjoyed as a youth. In 1974 Stone graduated from the University of Illinois with honors in Animal Science. After living in Mexico for five years, he later graduated from the National Autonomous University's College of Veterinary Medicine and moved to Florida. Over the years he has served as President of the South Florida Veterinary Medical Association, the Lake County Veterinary Medical Association, and as executive secretary for three national veterinary organizations. Dr. Stone is currently the Chief of Staff of the Veterinary Trauma Center of Groveland, an advanced-level care facility. In addition to lecturing internationally, he is the author of over seventy scientific articles and a number of Westerns, including *Trail Hand* (2006), *Badman's Pass*

(2016), and *Across the Río Bravo* (2017). Still a firearms collector, horse enthusiast, and now a black-belt-ranked martial artist, R. W. Stone presently lives in Central Florida with his wife, two daughters, one horse, and three dogs.

Center Point Large Print
600 Brooks Road / PO Box 1
Thorndike, ME 04986-0001 USA

(207) 568-3717

US & Canada:
1 800 929-9108
www.centerpointlargeprint.com